"WE'VE COME FOR BELLE STARR!"

"Then you've come to the wrong place," Mark Counter answered. "There's nobody answering to her description here."

"I'm willing to *believe* she hasn't told you who she is, Mr. Counter," the bounty hunter asserted. "But we *know* that blonde gal's Belle Starr and we're making a citizen's arrest, so's we can claim that reward put out by the bank in Wichita."

"That's not why *you* want her," Mark corrected. "You *know* she didn't do it."

"That's for the courts to decide, not us," the bounty hunter claimed. "We've no quarrel with *you*, just so long as you don't try to stand between us and our *legal* right to make a citizen's arrest."

"If that's what you want, come ahead," Mark replied, his voice even. "All you have to do is pass *me*!"

J.T. Edson

TEXAS TRIO

Originally Published in Great Britain as
Calamity, Mark and Belle

CHARTER BOOKS, NEW YORK

This book was originally published
in Great Britain under the
title *Calamity, Mark and Belle*.

This Charter book contains the complete
text of the original edition.
It has been completely reset in a typeface
designed for easy reading and was printed
from new film.

TEXAS TRIO

A Charter Book/published by arrangement with
Transworld Publishers, Ltd.

PRINTING HISTORY
Corgi edition published 1980
Charter edition/October 1989

ISBN: 1-55773-269-8

Charter Books are published by The Berkley Publishing Group,
200 Madison Avenue, New York, N.Y. 10016.
The name "CHARTER" and the "C" logo are trademarks belonging
to Charter Communications, Inc.

PRINTED IN THE UNITED STATES OF AMERICA

10 9 8 7 6 5 4 3 2 1

For Sue "the Catford Kid" Richards and Gordon Harrison, without whose help I couldn't get from here to there and back, with stops along the way.

Author's note:

The events recorded in this book previously appeared in a shortened form as, Part One, "The Bounty On Belle Starr's Scalp," TROUBLED RANGE. However, as the Counter family have at last agreed to allow the full story to be put into print, here it is. They stipulated it should be included in the "Calamity Jane" and not the "Floating Outfit" series. To save our "old hands" from repetition, but for the benefit of new readers, we have given details of the career and special qualifications of Miss Martha "Calamity Jane" Canary and Mark Counter in the form of appendices.

While we realize that in our present "permissive" society we could employ the actual profanities, we do not concede that a spurious desire for "realism" is any excuse to do so.

Lastly, as we do not pander to the current "trendy" usage of the metric system, we are continuing to say pounds, ounces, miles, yards, feet and inches where these are applicable.

J.T. Edson

Active Member, Western Writers of America,
MELTON MOWBRAY, Leics. England.

CHAPTER ONE

An Unusual Occupation

"Entschuldigen sie bitte, frauline. Sind sie die damen die dieses in der zeitung getan hat?"

"I'm afraid I can't understand you. Can't you-all speak English?"

Although Ernst Kramer was on his way to attend a business meeting with two of the men who acted as his agents west of the Mississippi River, when just as he was locking the door of his second floor suite of rooms, he heard his native tongue being spoken—albeit with a Prussian accent and not that of the Westphalian district from which his parents had emigrated to the United States of America while he was a child—he paused and looked towards the stairs leading down to the entrance lobby of the Columbus Grand Hotel.[1]

Even if there had been anybody else in sight, Kramer would have experienced no difficulty in deciding who had asked and who, in a negative way, had answered the question. There was not even any need to see the copy of the *Ellsworth Tribune* which was being displayed to supply a clue as to the identity of the first speaker. Everything about his physical appearance gave indications of his ethnic origins and, to a certain extent, his social background to anybody who knew what to look for. No matter what his present attire suggested as to his position in life now, his original station in life definitely had not been that of a railroad construction worker.

Around six foot in height, well built, not long into his

---

1. *As opposed to usage in the British Isles, in the United States of America, that section of a multi-story building which is at street level is referred to as the "first" and not the "ground" floor. J.T.E.*

thirties, the speaker had removed his hat to display closely cropped blond hair. His fairly handsome, clean shaven features were hard and, as the texture of his skin would never take a tan, they were reddened by considerable exposure to the elements. There were small scars on his cheeks of the kind that were left after the duels with sabres which were common amongst a certain class of the population in Germany. Furthermore, he had the straight backed, square shouldered carriage of one who had been subjected to the rigid military discipline for which the army of his country was noted.

About the same height, although he was nearly twice as old and had allowed his bulky frame to run somewhat to fat as a result of much good and easy living, Kramer's appearance suggested that he had similar "roots" to those of the speaker; if from a lower stratum of society. His florid, almost porcine features lacked the "duelling scars" almost mandatory among the upper-middle class and aristocracy of Germany, but he had a hearty, well fed air which contributed to the sobriquet, "*der Fleischer*"—"the Butcher"—given to him by his associates. He had on stylish and costly city clothes of the latest fashion, as might be expected of a guest at the best and most expensive hotel in the thriving trail end town of Ellsworth, Kansas. However, they neither flattered his physique, nor detracted from his all too obvious corpulence. Not even the best tailor in the world could achieve those kind of results when in contention with such a figure.

As Kramer frequently spoke German in the course of his everyday life, he translated the question mentally and did not need to give it conscious thought. His main attention was directed at the person to whom it was uttered. His gross appearance notwithstanding, he had always possessed a well developed interest in members of the opposite sex; particularly when they were physically attractive. So, listening to the answer—which was spoken in the fashion of a Southron who had had a good education and upbringing—he was far from averse to the opportunity of making her acquaintance. He had noticed her around the hotel several times since his arrival the previous afternoon and, although she did not entirely fulfil his standards for the ideal woman, he was willing to concede she came pretty close to it.

She appeared to be in her early twenties and stood around

five foot eight inches, somewhat taller than a great many men preferred. However, *der Fleischer's* tastes ran to junoesque proportions and she was on the verge of having those. Certainly she was far from being of slender and fragile build, which was the main reason he found her so pleasant to the eye.

If the severely masculine white silk blouse and dark blue necktie worn by the young woman were intended to conceal what lay beneath, they failed badly. Rather they enhanced the full, firm swell of her magnificent bosom and the way in which her torso trimmed to a slender waist. Nor was her plain black skirt any more successful in hiding her equally rich, curvaceous hips, which gave a hint that they joined shapely, if sturdy, legs. Taking her brunette hair back into a tight and unflattering bun, wearing horn-rimmed spectacles, and avoiding the employment of even the modest amount of make-up permissible for a "good" member of her sex—on the standards by which such things were judged west of the Mississippi River—such measures still could not obliterate the beauty of her sun bronzed face. Neither could her serious expression conceal the attractiveness of her features.

"Perhaps I could help you, ma'am?" Kramer offered, his accent was that of one who had been born and raised in Chicago, and yet it retained a harsh timbre that suggested his Teutonic birthright. Judging from the absence of any kind of jewellery on the young woman the description, *"fraulein,"* was correct with regards to her marital status, and while speaking, he swept off his pearl grey derby hat with what he imagined to be a gallant flourish; but which merely exhibited his balding greyish-brown hair. "I can speak German."

"Thank you, *sir*," the beautiful young woman replied, turning her gaze to *der Fleischer* and, although her tone was polite, there was also a noticeable hint of irritation rather than gratitude in it as she went on, "Could you tell me what this man wants, please?"

"Of course," Kramer obliged. "He asked if you are the lady who put something in the newspaper he is showing you."

"Well, yes. I do have an advertisement in it," the brunette admitted, running a far from complimentary—or enthusiastic —gaze over the poorly dressed blond. "In fact, although I don't see how it could *possibly* be of an interest to *him*, I believe it is the one to which he was pointing."

"Ah yes!" Kramer ejaculated, looking to where the younger man was still indicating a prominent item on the second page of the newspaper. He quickly read the information it contained. As he originated from a culture that still tended to restrict the roles in which women were supposed to participate, he could not prevent a slightly sardonic timbre from entering his voice as he continued, "So you are Miss Cornelia *von* Blücherdorf of Atlanta, Georgia, and you purchase, or offer expert valuations of jewellery, antiques, or *objet d'art*?"

"I am she, *sir*!" the young woman affirmed, her attitude suggesting defiance which was mingled with an air of also being defensive. "And, despite my *sex*—trusting my use of the word '*sex*' does not offend you, *sir*—I assure you that I am *very* competent at my work."

"That I don't doubt for a moment, ma'am," *der Fleischer* asserted hurriedly, guessing that her reactions were caused because she had found the need to require the assistance of a man. He still hoped to benefit from the situation and he adopted what he hoped would be regarded as a placatory demeanour. "Although you must admit it is a most unusual occupation for a wom—young lady."

"So is being a *prize fighter*, or whatever they are called!" Cornelia snapped, showing she was more annoyed than soothed by what a person with a greater sense of diplomacy than Kramer possessed would have regarded as a tactless comment; particularly in view of the conclusions he had drawn with regards to her outlook on the subject. "But I hear that there are *some* women who have taken up *that* unsavoury occupation and I doubt whether any of the *men* who crowd to see their disgusting exhibitions ever tell them it is *unusual*."

"Telling a woman pugilist such a thing could be dangerous," Kramer pointed out, with the kind of heavy-handed humour which appealed to him. He had spent the previous evening attending and enjoying the event to which he suspected the young woman was making an indirect reference. However, seeing that his attempt to introduce a lighter note in the conversation was not succeeding—rather the opposite, in fact—he went on in as close to a deferential manner as his nature allowed, "Anyway, if I might be of assistance to you now, I will be delighted to do so."

"Thank you, *sir*," Cornelia answered, although the way in which she employed the honorific gave no indication that she was mollified by the offer. Instead of taking advantage of it, in fact, her next words were directed at the younger man. "Don't you speak *any* English at all?"

"Ver' small," the blond confessed, in what passed as that language. Then he tapped the advertisement with the forefinger of his left hand, which was also holding his hat and went on hesitantly, as if having to think out the words. "But with—such a—name—you—speaking the *Deutsch, nein*?"

"He means that your name has led him to assume you would speak German, Miss *von* Blücherdorf," *der Fleischer* announced, his tone suggesting a similar thought had occurred to him.

"I *thought* it might!" Cornelia admitted shortly, yet there was something in her demeanour which prevented Kramer from giving up the attempt to become better acquainted and walking away. "But, as I merely took the name from my step-father, I don't—." While she refrained from adding, "Not that it is any of *your business*", the point was made obvious by her tone and attitude. Once more returning her attention to the younger man, she went on, "What is it you want of me?"

"*Ich*—I have—something—!" the blond began, making a gesture towards the right hand pocket of his jacket. The last two words of the sentence came out as, "haff zumthink" and were repeated, again without being taken anything further. Instead, frowning, he resumed in his native tongue by muttering, '*Welches ist der wort nach, 'wertvoll*'?"

"*Es ist* 'valuable'," Kramer offered.

"*Sprechen zie Deutsch*?" the younger man began, although *der Fleischer* considered his reaction to that possibility was somewhat less enthusiastic than might have been expected under the circumstances.

"Are *you Herr von* Blücherdorf?" the blond asked in German, but with a typically arrogant Prussian disbelief that a person like Kramer could have acquired the honorific "von" to his name.

"*Nein!*" *der Fleischer* denied.

"Her employer then?" suggested the young man, in the same superior way.

"Just a good friend," Kramer lied. "And, as she speaks no German, I will interpret for you."

"That won't be necessary!" the blond stated, exuding the kind of haughty manner *der Fleischer* had experienced before when dealing with members of the Prussian upper class. Then he put on his hat with an almost military precision, and turned towards the stairs.

"What was all that about?" Cornelia demanded, rather than asked, having been glancing from one man to the other throughout the brief exchange between them in their native tongue.

"From what he said," Kramer replied. "I think that he has something of value he wanted to show you."

"Then why doesn't—?" the girl asked. Then an expression of comprehension came to her beautiful face and she raised her voice, calling, "Hey, you there. Stop!"

"Halt!" *der Fleischer* barked, employing the tone he had found was most suitable for producing obedience from members of his race. On the order being obeyed, probably as a result of the discipline instilled during military service rather than through any genuine desire to oblige, he glanced at the girl in an interrogative fashion. "Do you want to speak with him?"

"I—I—!" Cornelia began and it was obvious to Kramer that her reluctance to appear needful of masculine assistance was struggling against her curiosity. Although the latter won, she finished in a voice which was still redolent of her mixed emotions. "Well, yes. I *do*. Would you ask him to show me whatever it is he's brought, please?"

"Of course!" Kramer promised and did so.

Instead of complying on receiving the translated request, the blond began to continue his interrupted departure. An angry exclamation burst from the girl and her right hand darted quickly into the functional rather than dainty black vanity bag which was swinging by its carrying strings from her left wrist. Before she could produce whatever it was for which she was reaching, two men appeared at the foot of the stairs and started to ascend.

"Fritz, Otto!" *der Fleischer* called in a commanding voice, then continued, still speaking German. "Come back here, my man. We haven't finished with you yet!"

Matching the blond in height, but built more on the lines of Kramer, the hang of the cheap suits worn by the men at the foot of the stairs showed their bulk was comprised of hard muscle and not fat. They were in their early twenties and obviously of Teutonic origins. On hearing what *der Fleischer* said, they came to a halt and their right hands went underneath the left sides of their jackets.

For a moment, it seemed that the blond intended to continue his departure. However, studying the threatening way in which the pair of brawny new arrivals were standing blocking the stairs, he gave a shrug of angry resignation and returned. Keeping their hands in concealment, the two young men resumed their advance and halted at the entrance of the passage.

"Here he is for you," Kramer announced with a smug air, looking at the girl.

"Thank you, sir," Cornelia replied and, still making no attempt to conceal her dislike for having to be reliant upon another person—and a man at that—for assistance, she went on, "Ask him what he wants, please."

"He says nothing," Kramer reported, having carried out the instruction. "He made a mistake."

"Ask him if it's the kind of mistake the town marshal would be interested in," the girl suggested, keeping her right hand inside the vanity bag.

When the question was put to him, the blond stiffened. For a moment, it appeared as though he was contemplating flight. However, after glancing over his shoulder to where the two burly young men were blocking access to the stairway and displaying the butts of the revolvers—which were tucked in the waistbands of their trousers—they were grasping, he once more gave a shrug. His voice was cold and angry as he looked to his front and addressed *der Fleischer*.

"What did he say?" Cornelia inquired, after a moment.

"That he would rather not speak with you out here in the passage," Kramer replied, having deliberately waited to make the girl request the information.

"Very well," Cornelia said, once more after a brief pause in which she frowned pensively prior to reaching what was clearly a decision. "Will you tell him that I'll take him to my room, please?"

"Yes," Kramer agreed, thinking of suggesting that his own quarters were used but deciding that the girl would be unlikely to concur. But he was determined to continue his participation in the affair. "That's what we'll do."

"*We?*" Cornelia repeated, showing suspicion.

"You're going to continue needing an interpreter," *der Fleischer* pointed out. "And it might be a wise precaution to have somebody else present in case he isn't here for what you believe, but has robbery—or worse—in mind."

"I'm quite capable of protecting myself, *sir!*" the brunette declared, making a slight gesture with the bag which was still concealing whatever she was grasping in her right hand. But there was a suggestion of uncertainty in her voice. Then, trying to convey the impression that she was reaching the decision on purely practical grounds and even conferring a favour by doing so, she continued, "Yet, in spite of that, an interpreter would come in useful I suppose, if——Very well, sir. If this man has no objections, you can come. Just *you*, of course, not your friends."

"My *men* might be useful—!" Kramer commenced, the emphasis he placed upon the second word indicating that the pair were merely his employees and he did not consider them as social equals, or friends.

"And, going by his behaviour, the matter he wants to see me about is almost certainly of a very—confidential—nature," Cornelia pointed out. "In which case, he wouldn't want too many people to know of it."

"Are we worried about what *he* wants?" Kramer inquired.

"I am, *sir!*" Cornelia asserted, returning to her original self-assured attitude. "And, as I've had far more experience in such matters than you-all, I'll be obliged if you will allow me to conduct this one in my own way."

"Whatever you say," Kramer surrendered. "But I think we'd be wise to let them stay in the corridor outside your door."

"That's all right with me," the girl assented, with the air of one conferring a favour. Releasing whatever she was holding, she brought her empty hand from the bag and continued, "I will, of course, reimburse you for your services as interpreter."

"That won't be necessary!" *der Fleischer* protested jovially.

"I consider it *most* necessary, *sir*!" Cornelia stated in a manner which warned she would not be swayed from the position she had taken. "In fact, I insist upon doing so."

"Very well," Kramer conceded, with an amiability he was far from feeling. He resented such a high handed attitude from a woman, but realized she was adamant and sufficiently stubborn, if he argued, to exclude him from participating in the matter any further. "It will be a pleasure to accept whatever reimbursement you feel I deserve."

"Thank you, sir," Cornelia answered, but less with gratitude than what *der Fleischer* guessed was a sullen and grudging acceptance of her inability to continue the negotiations without the assistance of a member of the opposite six. "Will you tell him to come with us to my room, please?"

There followed another brief conversation in German, with the girl looking on incomprehensively. At first, the blond appeared to be objecting to anybody other than her present. Then, having had something brusquely explained and that explanation being accompanied by a gesture to the two burly young men whose arrival had prevented his departure earlier, he yielded with bad grace to the suggestions Kramer had made.

"I presume he's agreeable?" Cornelia remarked, when the blond and *der Fleischer* looked at her.

"He is," Kramer confirmed, exuding the smug condescension of one who knew his services had proved indispensable. "He objected to me coming at first, but I told him you wouldn't allow a strange man in your room without there was a chaperone present. So he agreed."

"Does he know your men will be outside the door?" the girl asked.

"I told him they would be," *der Fleischer* answered. "So there's no need for you to be afraid."

"I am not *afraid*!" Cornelia snapped indignantly, once again making a gesture with the vanity bag now grasped in her left hand. "It's just that I consider having him know they will be close by is a sensible precaution. Come with me, please!"

"It will be a pleasure," Kramer replied, his far from prepossessing features not improved by their smug smirk. "I'm only too pleased to be of service to you."

Having the kind of outlook a later generation would refer to as that of a "male chauvinist pig," *der Fleischer* was deriving considerable satisfaction in the way circumstances had compelled the haughty young beauty—who he suspected of being in sympathy with, if not an actual participant of, the growing "feminist" movement to which his background and upbringing took great exception—to be dependant upon his assistance to conduct a business deal she would much have preferred to handle unaided.

CHAPTER TWO

I'm *In*, Or There's *No* Deal

Swinging on her heel, with her whole bearing and manner indicative of frustrated annoyance, Cornelia von Blücherdorf stalked—rather than merely walked—towards the last door on the left side of the second floor passage. Grinning triumphantly, Ernst Kramer ordered the sulky looking blond to accompany him and, with the two brawny young men bringing up the rear in a protective fashion, followed her. Unlocking and opening the door, she allowed *der Fleischer* and the blond to precede her into the room. With Kramer's employees obeying the instructions he had given to them, by halting in the passage on either side of the door, she entered and closed it behind her.

Unlike the more spacious quarters occupied by *der Fleischer* and his men, the brunette's room offered accommodation for only one person. For all that, it was furnished just as well and comfortably. Which was only to be expected of the best and most expensive hotel in Ellsworth, Kansas. Situated in a town which was drawing the majority of its income in one way or another from the numerous herds of cattle driven from Texas to its railroad's shipping pens, the kind of guests who could afford to stay at the Columbus Grand Hotel were sufficiently wealthy to demand a high standard of luxury.

The furnishings of Cornelia's room were all of excellent quality. There was a sizeable single bed, a sidepiece which could also be utilized as a dressing- or writing-table, a washstand complete with decoratively painted jug and matching bowl, a large wardrobe and two comfortable chairs. Its two windows looked out respectively upon the rear and the alley at the left side of the building. The latter was open and, hanging

11

upon a hook alongside it, partially concealed by the unclosed drapes, was a coiled rope to be used as a means of escape in case of an emergency such as a fire.

While the bed was made up and none of the girl's clothing was to be seen, on the sidepiece were indications of her occupation. Near a carafe filled with water, its top covered by a tumbler—both of which were the property of the hotel—a small hammer lay across a thin sheet of iron about a foot square. Next to them reposed a short, cylindrical black "loupe"; the kind of magnifying glass used especially by watchmakers or jewellers. There were three corn tongs of different sizes and a set of brass scales designed for the accurate weighing of very light items. This latter stood in its polished mahogany case and was sheltered beneath a glass dome to prevent its delicate operation from being affected by dust settling upon it. While of good quality, none of the equipment was new and all had seen considerable usage.

"Sit down, please!" Cornelia ordered rather than requested, making no attempt to hide her disapproval of the situation into which circumstances had forced her.

"He says he would rather stand," Kramer answered, and having passed on the grudgingly given invitation, he also refrained from accepting.

"As you will, it's all one to me," the brunette stated, crossing to close the window overlooking the alley and, taking the rope from its hook, she pushed it beneath the bed. Then she returned to where the men were standing and went on, "Ask him who he is and what he wants, please."

"His name is Franz *Schmidt*—or so he *says*," Kramer interpreted, having already acquired the information while watching the girl taking what he considered to be an ineffectual precaution against a departure by any means other than through the door. Nodding towards the buckskin pouch which the blond had taken from the right side pocket of the grubby and well worn jacket, he continued, "And *Herr Schmidt* thinks you might find the contents of that most interesting."

"Good heavens!" Cornelia breathed, having accepted, unfastened, opened and tipped some of the pouch's contents into the cupped palm of her left hand.

"*Gott in Himmel!*" der Fleischer ejaculated, far more loudly, at almost the same moment. Although he had reverted

instinctively to the language of his forebears, as he often did
when subjected to some strong emotion, he resumed speaking
English as he inquired, "Are they *real*?"

The cause of the exclamations were the dozen jewels which
the girl was holding. Three had the rich green coloration of
good quality emeralds. Another two were the blood red sheen
of rubies. Two more had the deep purpleviolet hue of ame-
thysts. One displayed the nacreous lustre of a pearl and the
remainder showed the crystalline glitter associated with diamonds. While none of them were of spectacular dimensions,
every one was of moderate size. Furthermore, they were not
the entire contents of the pouch.

"I don't know until I've carried out some tests," Cornelia
replied, trying without any great success to sound and appear
disinterested. "But there are quite a few more in here. Ask
him what he wants of me—please."

"He wants to sell them," Kramer explained for the blond,
his smallish eyes glinting with something more than casual
interest.

"Then would you ask him how they came into his possession?" the brunette requested, rolling the jewels around almost
sensually in her palm.

"He *says* that his mother left them to him in her will and
they've only just reached him," *der Fleischer* supplied from
the information he was given by the blond.

"It doesn't sound likely, but it *could* be true," Cornelia
commented and, without asking for proof of the story, went
on, "Will he let me make the necessary tests to ensure they
are genuine?"

"He says he's no objections," Kramer translated.

"Good!" the brunette said and, followed by the men,
walked over to the sidepiece.

Fitting the loupe into her right eye, Cornelia picked up the
smallest of the corn tongs. Using them with deft ease, she
selected one of the diamonds and gave it a close examination.
Replacing it, but making no comment to the watching men,
she subjected one of each other type of stone in turn to an
equally careful scrutiny.

"Well," *der Fleischer* asked, when the brunette laid down
the tongs and removed the loupe, displaying an impatience
which went far beyond that of one who was merely intending

to do a service as interpreter with no thought of monetary gain. "*Are* they real?"

"They certainly look as if they might be," Cornelia replied, frowning pensively. Here gaze went briefly to the sullen-looking blond, giving particular attention to his hand which—although Kramer had not noticed—appeared to be surprisingly clean and well kept for one whose attire gave the impression he was employed to perform hard manual labour. "He said they'd only just reached him, didn't he?"

"Yes."

"Will you ask him where they came from, please?"

"He says that his family's lawyers in Dusseldorf sent them to him as they were instructed in his mother's will," *der Fleischer* informed the girl, relaying the explanation he was given by the blond after what had obviously been a pause in which to think. "They were waiting for him with the rest of the mail at the railroad depot when he came in from the construction camp and, as he wants to set himself up in business instead of staying as a section hand, he wants to sell them."

"That would be the 'Dusseldorf' in Germany?" Cornelia said, half to herself.

"I've never heard of one over here," Kramer answered. "Why?"

"These stones have all been removed from their settings not too long ago."

"More recently than if they'd been sent all the way from Germany?"

"It's possible."

"Then he's *lying*!"

"I wouldn't go so far as to say *that*," Cornelia declared, then went on in the fashion of one who was trying to justify a dubious action to her conscience, "Of course, I may be wrong about how long it is since they were removed. It's hard to say definitely without more exhaustive tests than I've conducted. Will you ask him why he decided to bring them to me, instead of taking them to Isaac Jacobstein's jewellery shop. He must have passed it on his way here from the railroad depot."

"*Er ist eine Jude!*" Schmidt barked when the question was posed. His attitude indicating he thought this to be a sufficient reason, but he said something more while gesticulating with the copy of the *Ellsworth Tribune*.

"He says he doesn't want to do business with a Jew," Kramer explained. "And, as he saw you had a good German name, he came to you."

Although he had no intention of raising the point, *der Fleischer* realized there could be something more than just those reasons for the blond to have preferred the brunette instead of the local jeweller. Such a prejudice was common among the German people in general and the upper classes in particular and he could accept that a man with the kind of social background from which he was convinced 'Schmidt' had originated, might be disinclined to deal with Jacobstein on the grounds of what would become known as anti-semitism. On the other hand, apart from having seen her name and believing that she would speak his native tongue, there could have been another motive for him to seek out Cornelia von Blücherdorf.

Her sex!

If the jewels had been acquired illegally, which seemed possible considering the way in which the blond had become compliant when the girl mentioned the town marshal and in view of her speculations about how recently they had been removed from their settings, he might have decided it would be easier to fool her than a man with the story of how they had come into his possession.

This was a point of view which Kramer could understand, having a similar mentality.

"Yes!" Cornelia said, showing relief and trying to sound as if she was satisfied with the explanation. "I can understand how he would under *those* circumstances. I'll go on with the tests."

Placing the stones and pouch near the scales, the brunette took a small wooden box from a drawer of the sidepiece. On being opened, this proved to contain what appeared to be examples of various types of jewels.

"He wants to know what they're for," Kramer interpreted a question put in a suspicious tone by Schmidt.

"Comparison purposes," Cornelia replied, taking a nacreous globe from the box. "What would you say this is?"

"A pearl," Kramer declared without hesitation.

"It's a fake," the brunette corrected, raising the globe to her mouth. "Watch." Placing it between her teeth, she bit and it shot on to the sidepiece. Tossing it into the box, she repeated the experiment with the pearl from Schmidt's collection. This stayed in place and, having removed and returned it to the other jewels, she explained, "Mine was glass, which is smooth. A genuine article is rough enough, even though you can't see with the naked eye, for your teeth to be able to grip it."

"Let me try," *der Fleischer* demanded rather than requested and, without waiting for permission, duplicated the girl's actions with the same results. "You're right."

"I *never* doubted *that* for a moment!" Cornelia answered, returning to her earlier attitude of indignation. "*May* I continue?"

"Go to it!" Kramer assented.

"This should convince you I *know* what I'm talking about!" Cornelia asserted, picking up and placing the fake pearl on the metal plate. On being struck by the hammer, it shattered and she indicated the pieces, saying. "I'd hardly do that with a real one, would I? If you'd like to examine the remains through my loupe—."

"No," Kramer refused. "Like you said, you wouldn't bust up a real pearl. How about the rest of them, though?"

"I'll *see*!" the brunette promised, making it plain she resented the attempt to rush her.

In spite of his earlier cynicism with regards to Cornelia's claim to be engaged upon what *der Fleischer* considered was a masculine type of work and therefore beyond the capability of a woman; she proved to be very competent. It soon became apparent that she was determined to prove her qualifications in the field. As she was carrying out the examinations, she explained the special qualities of the different types of stones and how the testing of each was performed.

Filling the tumbler with water from the carafe, the brunette demonstrated how—as she asserted would happen—the fake amethyst from her box lost most of its colour when submerged. On the other hand, the stone from the collection belonging to Schmidt retained its rich purpleviolet sheen. Her tests of the emeralds and rubies were equally adequate and convincing.

However, the most dramatic exhibition came with the diamonds!

"Can you tell this from the real thing?" Cornelia challenged, picking the crystalline fake from the box with the corn tongs.

"It looks just the same as——!" Kramer replied, reaching out.

"Don't touch it!" Cornelia ordered, preventing *der Fleischer* from doing so by jerking the tongs clear of his outstretched hand. "One of the ways *we* can differentiate between a real and an imitation diamond is by the warmth to the touch. Glass conducts heat less readily than most crystals and so it feels warmer to the touch. Which is why I'm holding it with the tongs. To use the bare hands would raise the stone's temperature and vitiate the test."

"Let me try," Kramer requested, after the brunette had conducted the test and pronounced Schmidt's diamond genuine.

"Very well," Cornelia assented, offering the tongs which held the two stones, with a superior smile.

"They both taste the same to me," Kramer protested, having duplicated the application of each in turn to his tongue.

"I'm not surprised," Cornelia declared, making no attempt to conceal her satisfaction over the abortive attempt. "It's a knack *we* jewellers acquire and the *ordinary* person rarely manages to pick up. However, there are ways somebody like *you* can tell the real from the fake."

"I've heard a real diamond will cut glass," Kramer said, annoyed by the way in which he had been addressed by a mere woman.

"It will," the brunette confirmed, but in a tone redolent of sarcasm. "Of course, to make such a test, one must have a suitable piece of glass present; or either spoil something of one's own, like the face of one's watch, or one could chance annoying the owner by making the test on a window, or something else, which is handy."

"Then how do you do it?" *der Fleischer* inquired, his hackles rising at the complete lack of respect he was being accorded and to which he was not accustomed when dealing with members of the "weaker" sex.

"Quite simply," Cornelia replied, taking the crystalline stone from her box.

Placing the small object on the iron plate, the brunette took the hammer and gave it a sharp blow. As had happened with the imitation pearl, it was shattered by the impact. However, although she had refrained on the earlier experiment, she swept aside the fragments and replaced them with one of the glistening pieces from the collection belonging to Schmidt.

"What is she—?" the blond demanded in a mixture of indignation and alarm, as the hammer was raised, remembering that a similar experiment had not been made with the pearl from the pouch.

Before the question could be completed, or its maker was able to intervene, Cornelia struck the stone if anything somewhat harder than she had either the supposed diamond or fake pearl. However, instead of being splintered into pieces, the glistening stone proved to have remained intact when the hammer rebounded from it. In fact, the only evidence that it had been hit with considerable force was a new mark added to those which already marred the sheet of metal.

"Whew!" Kramer ejaculated, staring at the unaffected stone. "That had him *worried*!"

"Tell *him* a diamond is the hardest substance known to man," the brunette instructed, in a tone suggesting she had nothing other than contempt for anybody who was unaware of such a basic scientific fact and she included *der Fleischer* in that category. "You-all could hit a real diamond far harder than I did without causing it the slightest damage."

"So they *are* genuine?" Kramer breathed.

"Those I've examined so far definitely are," the girl confirmed with complete assurance. "But I intend to check the rest before I'm satisfied."

"Go ahead!" Kramer said, as if conferring a favour from a position of authority instead of agreeing in the minor capacity of interpreter.

"*Thank you!*" Cornelia replied, showing she had noticed the distinction.

Going to one of the chairs, *der Fleischer* sat down and watched the brunette set about subjecting the rest of the stones from the pouch to the tests by which she had established the validity of the first batch. He also kept an eye upon Schmidt. At first, the blond paid just as much attention to the examination. Then he began to pace up and down the room restlessly. Although while doing so, he kept approaching one or other of the windows, Kramer felt no concern over his perambulations.

Der Fleischer was confident that the blond did not contemplate flight, but was merely growing impatient. It was unlikely he would be willing to leave his property behind, or try to retrieve it before departing as he knew there were two armed men outside who could arrive quickly enough to prevent him. The likelihood of his doing so decreased, in Kramer's opinion, as the tests continued upon the considerable number of stones without there being any indication of them being other than genuine.

"They're real all right!" Cornelia declared at last, returning the stones to the pouch. "Ask him how much he wants for them, please."

"Twenty thousand dollars," Kramer quoted at the blond's request.

"They're worth at least that much," Cornelia declared, sounding disinterested and just a trifle perturbed. "Tell him I'll give him *ten* thousand."

"He say no," *der Fleischer* reported, although Schmidt's attitude as he barked out the word, *"Nein!"* had been sufficient proof of his refusal.

"Tell him in that case, he is quite at liberty to go to Isaac Jacobstein, or elsewhere," Cornelia suggested with icy calm. "Then say that, like myself, *whoever* he goes to will know that the *Comtesse de* Saint-Pierre would be delighted to—buy —them."

On delivering the message, Kramer saw the blond stiffen as he repeated the name mentioned by the brunette. While it meant nothing to him, he could see the same did not apply to Schmidt. In fact, such was the reaction, that for a moment he wished he was armed and he contemplated calling in his two men from the passage. However, after darting frustrated glances from the door to each of the windows in turn and to where the rope had been concealed beneath the bed, the blond gave a shrug of bitter resignation. Glaring at Cornelia in obvious hatred, he made a counter offer in a way which suggested he doubted whether it would be accepted.

"He says he'll take fifteen thousand," Kramer interpreted. "But I don't think he expects to get it."

"That's fortunate for him," Cornelia declared. "Because you can tell him ten thousand is the absolute limit I'm willing to go to."

Despite the brunette's manner implying she was satisfied that she held all the winning cards, *der Fleischer* could not help thinking, as he was relaying her terms, that there was something making her uneasy. In fact, she struck him as being more concerned and worried than the situation appeared to warrant.

"He accepts," Kramer announced.

"Tell him I'll give him—a thousand dollars—now," Cornelia suggested. "And we will leave the pouch in the hotel's safe until I get the balance."

"He doesn't care for the idea," Kramer translated. "In fact, he says he wants the full sum, cash on the barrelhead."

"I haven't the authority to draw so mu—!" Cornelia protested, but brought the comment to a halt and, after a slight pause, she made a revision as if hating to have to say the words, "I've over-spent my budget and have to send to my step-father for more. The authorization to draw it will be here by tomorrow evening at the latest."

"He says he can't wait and must have the money straight away," Kramer stated, in response to Schmidt's reply to the proposal. "Shall I tell him you can't pay and he may as well go?"

A feeling of elation welled within *der Fleischer*. It was produced by a combination of the discovery that the arrogant young woman was not sufficiently trusted by her step-father to handle large sums of money at will and an appreciation of how her predicament could be of benefit to him. The latter thought was what had motivated his question.

"No, you will *not*!" Cornelia stated grimly, placing the pouch into which she had returned the stones on the sidepiece and setting her hands on her hips in a gesture of defiance. "He came to *me* and you-all just *happened* to be available. So you're not going off with him to buy the jewels for yourself. Either I'm *in*, or there's *no* deal!"

"How big a part can you take?" Kramer asked.

Just as *der Fleischer* had sensed earlier from Schmidt's attitude that any further attempt at reducing the price would be resisted, so he knew the brunette was equally adamant. As trying to impose a lesser amount could have ended in a disturbance which brought in the local peace officers and saw the removal of the jewels, cutting her out of the deal would produce a similar effect. Rather than miss such a great opportunity, Kramer was willing to swallow his resentment of a woman invading masculine preserves and allow her to save face by participating.

"All I can raise is fifteen hundred dollars," Cornelia replied sourly.

"Then I'll put up the rest," *der Fleischer* declared. "I'll send one of my men to collect the money from the bank. It will only take a few minutes and I think our friend Schmidt can wait that long to be paid."

CHAPTER THREE

Somebody Could Get Killed

"Well, here's *my* share of the money at last!" Ernst Kramer announced in a satisfied tone, his look of satisfaction doing nothing to improve his florid features, as he turned after closing the door of Cornelia von Blücherdorf's room. "*Now* we can conclude this business and let *Herr—Schmidt*—be on his way."

Some fifteen minutes had elapsed since *der Fleischer* had dispatched one of his employees to the First National Bank, telling the other in a loud voice to remain in the passage outside the door. He had given his emissary a note of authorization to collect the cash box, which he had deposited there on his arrival in Ellsworth from Chicago, and to return with it to the Columbus Grand Hotel as quickly as possible. Despite the short distance involved, this had taken somewhat longer than anticipated.

While she and her two clearly far from welcome guests were waiting, the brunette had produced the fifteen hundred dollars which was all she was able to contribute to the purchase price of the jewels brought by the man who Kramer had made it obvious he did not believe was born with the plebian name of "Franz Schmidt." Then they had reached an agreement, not without some debate, upon the amount of the stones to which this sum entitled her.

Despite showing her dissatisfaction over the way things had gone, Cornelia had unbent sufficiently to explain to Kramer why her reference to the "*Comtesse de* Saint-Pierre" had caused the Germanic-looking blond to accept far less than the actual value for the contents of the pouch. The woman in question was a very wealthy European aristocrat whose collection of jewellery—all internationally known pieces, although not of exceptional quality—had disappeared while she was paying a visit to New York a few weeks earlier. The chief suspect had been the *Comtesse's* maid, due to her having formed a liaison with a handsome young Prussian alleged to have been a former officer in the German Army who had been cashiered as a result of an unspecified scandal. Although protesting her innocence, the maid had already tried to commit suicide when she discovered the man had taken his departure. Because of the victim's social prominence, details of the theft had not been public by the New York Police Department. However, the Pinkerton National Detective Agency—into whose hands the case had been put by the *Comtesse*—had privately circulated a description of the pieces taken to all respectable jewellers and, in all probability, other dealers who did not qualify for inclusion in such a category.

Being aware of the theft and the clandestine publicity it had received throughout the jewellery trade, when her examination had suggested that the stones had been removed from their settings in an amateurish fashion, the brunette had suspected they could be part of the *Comtesse's* purloined collection. In spite of her summation, having either a streak of larceny of being desirous of proving her business acumen, she had overlooked the possibility that she might be dealing in stolen property. *Der Fleischer* was inclined to the latter motive. Furthermore, having been informed of her suspicions, he had not seen fit to withdraw from the arrangement. All he was concerned with had been the thought that he stood to make a substantial profit out of the deal which, through no fault of her own and in spite of her wishes for it to be otherwise, she was unable to consummate without his assistance.

At last, a knock on the door heralded the arrival of the messenger. Accepting the sizable metal cash box which was offered to him, Kramer had repeated his command for his employees to remain in the immediate vicinity of the room. Then he had turned to set about closing the deal.

"I suppose we can!" Cornelia agreed, pivoting around from the window overlooking the alley at which she had been standing, presumably to watch for the young man's return from the bank. Crossing to the sidepiece, she was still clearly far from enamoured of the comparatively minor part circumstances were compelling her to play in what otherwise would have been a most lucrative negotiation. "If you-all will count out your *share*, sir, I'll take the stones you're allowing me to purchase."

"Go ahead," *der Fleischer* authorized, with a hearty joviality which a more sensitive man would have guessed was unlikely to bring an improvement to the brunette's disposition.

Unlocking the cash box with the small key attached to the fob of his ostentatiously massive gold watch chain, Kramer took out a thick wad of currency and began to count as he peeled banknotes from it. Nevertheless, while doing this, he also kept his eye upon Cornelia as she removed and set aside the small quantity of the jewels which they had decided would be her share. With the division completed, still showing signs of disappointment and annoyance, she returned the remainder. Closing the buckskin pouch, she secured its neck by fastening the drawstring with a complicated and over-sized bow.

Just as *der Fleischer* was handing over the eight thousand five hundred dollars which was his contribution to the purchase price, something happened to jolt him from the complacent frame of mind!

The kind of yell associated with a charge by the cavalry of the Confederate States' Army during the War of Secession— and still much used by celebrating Texas' cowhands—rang out!

It originated from the alley at the left side of the Columbus Grand Hotel! However, rowdy and unexpected though it was, the whoop alone did not cause the consternation which ensued!

A revolver crashed from the same direction as the yell and an upper pane of the window which Cornelia had closed, as a precaution against Schmidt trying to leave that way, was shattered by the bullet!

The bullet and not the yell produced the various reactions from the occupants of the room!

Giving vent to a profanity in German, *der Fleischer* nevertheless slammed down the lid of the cash box and caused its automatic lock to operate before he looked in the appropriate direction!

Showing an equally instinctive concern for the welfare of what had just become his property, Schmidt thrust the money he had been given hurriedly into the right hand pocket of his jacket before he too gave his attention to the damaged window!

However, while less noticeable, the incident created the most remarkable effect where the brunette was concerned!

A startled scream burst from Cornelia and she spun around!

From what happened next, it seemed the response was motivated by something other than fear!

The moment her back was turned to the two men, the brunette's hands began to move with great rapidity. They disappeared simultaneously into a pair of carefully concealed pockets in her skirt. On returning to view an instant later, the right no longer held the buckskin pouch.

Instead, Cornelia's left fist was grasping one which looked identical in every way, even to being fastened in the same distinctive manner!

The way in which her movements were carried out implied the brunette had had sufficient presence of mind to take advantage of a fortuitous distraction.

Or, considering that she had been in possession of a pouch suitable for making the exchange on her person, Cornelia had expected the distraction to occur!

Whichever was the case, such was the smoothly coordinated speed and dexterity with which the substitution had been made, it was clearly a trick resulting from considerable practise!

Transferring the duplicate pouch to her right hand, unnoticed by the two men as they dashed past her in the direction of the broken window, the brunette followed them. As she was doing so, the door was thrown open with considerable violence. Holding their imported, short barrelled, Webley Royal Irish Constabulary revolvers ready for use and demanding in German to be told what had happened, Kramer's employees dashed into the room from the passage. Looking over his shoulder and showing a commendable appreciation of the potential danger to his well being created by the latest developments, Schmidt sought to establish his innocence by thrusting his empty hands hurriedly into the air.

"Great merciful *heavens*!" Cornelia gasped, but the suggestion of alarm in her voice was not in accord with the way she had just behaved. As Kramer snarled in their native tongue for his employees to refrain from taking any offensive action against the blond she asked, "Whatever is *happening*. Are we being attacked by marauding *Indians*?"

"God damned beef heads!" *der Fleischer* spat out furiously in English and went on just as heatedly, but making no attempt to elaborate upon the meaning of the term he had used for the benefit of the brunette. "Somebody could get killed, the way those 'mother-something' sons-of-bitches go shooting their guns off.[1] The marshal should disarm every single bastard of them as soon as they come into town."

There was some justification for Kramer's heated and profane employment of the derogatory name for a Texan, particularly one who earned his living from the cattle industry which had brought that great State back to financial stability after its near ruinous participation on the side of the "South" during the War of Secession.[2] Two men, whose attire suggested they qualified for the unflattering classification—one of whom was carrying a revolver with smoke still curling from its muzzle—had been seen disappearing hurriedly around the corner at the rear end of the building as he had arrived at the window.

"I don't understand, sir," Cornelia protested.

"It was one of those 'mother-something' cowboys fooling about with his gun!" *der Fleischer* explained, with little reduction in his rancour, as was befitting for one who—without possession of the necessary requirements for enrollment, if the truth had been known—was prominent in the activities of the leading Chicago chapter of the Grand Army of the Republic.[3] "Those god-damned Johnny Rebs should *never* be let wear guns!"

"I can't say I approve of your *language*, sir, nor of the way you speak about our fellow supporters of the Southern cause!"

1. See the third paragraph of our "Author's Note". J.T.E.

2. What led to the improvement in the finances of Texas is told, at least in part, in: GOODNIGHT'S DREAM (Bantam Books, U.S.A. 1974 edition re-titled, despite Corgi Books having already published a different volume with that title in the United Kingdom, THE FLOATING OUTFIT) FROM HIDE AND HORN and SET TEXAS BACK ON HER FEET (Berkley Medallion Books, U.S.A. 1978 edition re-titled, VIRIDIAN'S TRAIL) J.T.E.

3. "Grand Army of the Republic": an association of Union Army and Navy veterans of the War of Secession, organized in 1866 in honour of the dead and to aid the widows and dependants of their comrades-in-arms who were killed in the conflict. J.T.E.

the brunette stated, her accent becoming even more pronounced. However, glancing at the shattered pane of the window, she went on with just a trifle less disapproval. "Although I must admit I'm inclined to agree with you-all about the dangerous way in which some of those Texans will fool around with their guns when they're in town. Here you are, sir."

"Thank you," Kramer replied, showing signs of being mollified by the girl's last four words and the action with which they were accompanied. Accepting the pouch she was offering, he tossed it up into the air a couple of times in a manner redolent of smug self satisfaction and went on in a more amiable voice, "That advertisement you put in the newspaper's paid off *very* well."

If *der Fleischer* had been less enthusiastic about the coup which he believed he had pulled off, putting the brunette in her place while doing so, he might have noticed that her reference to the behaviour of Texans implied a greater knowledge of the subject than should have been the case. As it was, having no idea that the substitution of pouches had even been contemplated—much less carried out—he did not bother to examine the contents of the one with which he was playing before putting it into the right hand pocket of his jacket.

"For *you*, sir, at any rate!" Cornelia pointed out sulkily, or at least exhibiting what appeared to be a feeling of bitter resentment. "Thank you for your *help*. However, in view of the circumstances, I hardly consider I'm under any obligation to reimburse you-all for your services as interpreter."

"I wouldn't expect it," Kramer asserted jovially, still making no attempt to conceal his elation over what he felt sure had been a most profitable piece of business thrown his way by chance. "In fact, I think it's only fair that I should pay *you* a commission for putting me in the way of buying these."

"Why that's *most* generous of you, sir!" Cornelia enthused, appearing to thaw a trifle in spite of *der Fleischer* having patted the pocket in a delighted gesture which should have served as a reminder to her of how her inability to speak German had produced the resultant offer. "The usual commission I would charge for such a transaction is five percent of the purchase price, but as you didn't pay it in full—!"

"Five hundred it is," Kramer interrupted, pleased with the

change which had come to the brunette's demeanour and seeking to cause an even further improvement, walking across the room in the direction of the sidepiece. "I'll put these away and get it for you straight away."

"Well, everything is settled," Schmidt said in tones of impatience, having taken the money from the pocket into which he had stuffed it and placed it into his wallet. He glanced to where the two burly young men, still holding their revolvers, were standing by the door. "Can I go now?"

"You can," Kramer asserted without consulting Cornelia, the question having been posed to him. Jerking his head in a gesture of dismissal, he continued to speak German as he addressed his employees. "Let *Herr—Schmidt—*pass and put those guns away. You don't need them."

"I don't think it would be—advisable—to talk about our transaction to *too* many people," Cornelia remarked, after the blond had departed, watching *der Fleischer* depositing the pouch in his cash box. "Not that I *doubt* the truth of the explanation he gave us for how they came into his possession of course."

"Or me, otherwise I wouldn't have bought them from him," Kramer seconded, showing no greater sincerity than had been in the brunette's voice. Having been thanked for the five hundred dollars he had counted from the still sizeable bundle in the box, he suggested hopefully, "Now perhaps you'll allow me to take you for lunch as a further token of my gratitude?"

"Not *lunch* I'm afraid," Cornelia refused, but with much better grace than she had exhibited at any time up to that point throughout their brief association. "I'm busy until this evening, but perhaps we could have *dinner* together?"

"That won't be possible either, I'm sorry to say," *der Fleischer* apologized. "I have to catch the east-bound train at four o'clock this afternoon."

There was a note of interrogation in Kramer's voice. It was caused by believing he had detected, through the way in which the brunette had worded her invitation, a suggestion that there might be more involved than merely taking an evening meal together. While he was willing for her to be his guest at lunch, as doing so would give him the opportunity later of boasting how easily the arrogant Southron "feminist" had discarded her principles because of receiving the commission of five hundred dollars, he was disinclined to delay his departure without being given more definite proof that staying overnight would be worthwhile.

"What a *pity*," Cornelia declared, returning the box with the imitation jewellery to the drawer from which it had been taken. "Oh well, it can't be helped. Perhaps we'll meet again some time and then I'll be able to take you up on your kind offer."

"It could be we might at that," Kramer conceded, concluding the requisite proof had not been given and that nothing further was going to result from the chance acquaintance. "I have to travel around a fair bit in my line of business."

"And so do I in mine," Cornelia pointed out, but showing none of the defensively aggressive stuffiness which had been in evidence earlier. "If you should ever be in Atlanta, Georgia, please feel free to come visit with me at my stepfather's shop—or at my *home*."

"Thank you, I'll do *that*," Kramer promised, tucking the cash box under his left arm and holding out his right hand. "Well, I'll have to be on my way."

In spite of having noticed how the invitation had been made, *der Fleischer* had refrained from duplicating the offer by suggesting that the brunette came to his home when she next found herself in Chicago. The nature of the business from which he derived the vast majority of his income was such that it made supplying his address to chance acquaintances inadvisable. In fact, such was his caution where the information was concerned that he had only written the name and location of his business premises when filling in the register at the hotel's reception desk on his arrival.

"Goodbye, sir," Cornelia replied, making no attempt to elicit further information and shaking hands in a firm manner indicative of considerable physical strength. "And, if you-all will excuse me for saying it *again*, if I was you, I'd be *very* careful who I let see those jewels for some time to come."

"And not the Pink-eyes, or the *Comtesse de* Saint-Pierre even after that time?" *der Fleischer* suggested, accompanying the employment of the derogatory name for operatives of the Pinkerton National Detective Agency with a wink to emphasise his heavily Teutonic wit.

"I really can't think *what* you-all mean, sir!" the brunette
asserted, but her right eyelid dipped and rose in a conspirator-
ial fashion. "Goodbye and thank you again for my commission."

"It was a pleasure to pay it," Kramer claimed, accepting
what was an obvious—if friendly—dismissal and, having
just realized that his hostess had not learned his name, decided
to depart before she should attempt to rectify the omission. In
view of her overt admission that she was sure the jewels had
been stolen, he felt the less she knew about him the better.
"Goodbye, Miss von Blücherdorf."

Waiting until *der Fleischer* and his men had taken their
departure, Cornelia crossed the room to the window with the
broken pane. Smiling in a way which removed the severity
from her features and showed she possessed a vivacity she had
kept hidden until that moment, she raised the bottom half and
leaned out.

Two men were standing in the alley with the blond. Tall,
lean, with deeply tanned features suggesting they had Indian
as well as white blood in their veins, each had a knife and a
revolver on his gun belt. They were the pair who had provoked, incorrectly, Kramer's angry comments about Texans as
a result of the distraction caused by the shot one of them had
fired. Smiling broadly, the blond raised his right hand in response to the brunette's wave. Then he accompanied his companions in the same direction they had taken earlier, but at a
more leisurely pace.

Lowering the window, Cornelia collected the coiled rope
—the removal of which had served to notify her accomplices
in the alley that the intended victim had entered the trap—and
returned it to its hook. Then, going to the sidepiece, she took
the pouch from the concealed pocket in her skirt. Replacing
the gems which she had been allowed to "purchase" in it, she
refastened the neck in a less distinctive fashion. Taking it and
the five hundred dollars she had received as her "commission"
to the wardrobe, she placed them in the somewhat larger than
usual plain black reticule which had been hanging inside.
With this done, she lifted out and donned a jacket which
matched the skirt.

"It serves you right, you arrogant son-of-a-bitch," the
brunette said softly, but with relish, thinking of the shock

which was awaiting Kramer when he discovered the substitution had taken place. "When you-all find out you've been rooked by the old 'diamond switch',[1] you're going to wish you hadn't been so all-fired eager to sell me short just because I'm a woman."

1. *A description of how another "team" tried to carry out the "diamond switch" confidence trick and the consequences when it failed is given in:* THE GENTLE GIANT. *J.T.E.*

CHAPTER FOUR

Kramer Will Be Gone by That Time

"Well now, Cousin Ezra, will you just lookee here?"

"I sure am looking, Cousin Abednego. It seems's how the Good Lord's considering us plumb favourable, what he's done sent our way!"

By the time the girl who had called herself "Cornelia von Blücherdorf"—but, in reality, bore a much more well known name—arrived in the second floor passage, Ernst Kramer and his two henchmen had already disappeared into their suite of rooms. Darting a glance at its closed door, she descended to the ground floor. Crossing the lobby, without handing her key to the clerk behind the reception desk in passing, she walked out of the Colombus Grand Hotel and along the street.

The brunette was convinced that the "diamond switch" confidence trick had been carried through without a hitch, or a hint of suspicion on the part of the victim. Nor did she doubt that, provided they were not subjected to tests similar to those she had made to establish the validity of the genuine stones, the "jewels" in *der Fleischer's* possession could be examined without betraying what had taken place during the distraction. For all that, she had been disinclined to take unnecessary chances. Therefore, on leaving the hotel, her actions would have suggested to any competent peace officer who had observed them that she was taking measures against the possibility of being followed.

Turning left on reaching the street, "Cornelia" walked only a short distance before making a gesture implying she had changed her mind. Then she reversed her direction. Meeting none of the people she had seen while leaving the hotel, she glanced into the entrance lobby as she was passing and satisfied herself that neither Kramer nor his bodyguards were in sight. She had not relied solely upon those precautions to make sure nobody was on her trail. While strolling along in an apparently aimless manner, she had on three occasions paused ostensibly to look at the goods displayed in the windows of stores she was passing. In actual fact, she was conducting a thorough examination of the street behind her. To avoid making her purpose too obvious, each time she had been careful to select premises offering wares which would appeal to members of her sex.

When satisfied that she was not being subjected to surveillance, the brunette left the "better" part of Ellsworth. However, she did not go far in the guise by which she had emerged from the hotel.

Despite her pose of having only recently arrived in the West from Atlanta, Georgia, "Cornelia" was aware that the district through which she must pass was not one a "good" woman would be advised to traverse alone after dark. Nor would it be entirely safe to do so in the daytime if such transitory visitors as cowhands from trail drives, railroad construction workers, or buffalo hunters, were celebrating. Everything had been comparatively quiet as she drew near, with none of the ribald rowdiness which would have warned her that some of the customers in the various places of entertainment were sufficiently drunk to forget the behaviour convention west of the Mississippi River with regard to women of her apparent social standing. For all that, she had no wish to attract attention by walking along dressed in such a fashion.

Going to a secluded spot between two buildings, which had served a similar purpose on previous occasions, "Cornelia" had quickly and effectively rectified the situation. Putting down her reticule, after having made sure there was nobody to observe her, she had started by taking off and laying aside the jacket. Stripping off her necktie, she had removed the collar and unfastened the shirt so it opened until almost at an indecorous level. By tugging at first one and then the other sleeve, she had caused them to part company from the rest of the garment. Then she had loosened the bun and shook out her hair to give it a less well groomed appearance. With all that done, she had produced some cheap jewellery from the reticule and tucked the discarded portions of the shirt into it.

Gathering up the jacket, which she would need to cover her bare arms before returning to the hotel, she had resumed her journey.

Simple as it had been, the effect of the transformation was remarkable. Gone was the staid and severe expression. Even without having applied any make-up, her demeanour and the hip-rolling walk she adopted made the brunette appear little different from any saloon-girl or prostitute who might be in the area.

However, in spite of "Cornelia's" efforts, the comments which were uttered as she was walking through an alley separating a saloon from a dancehall warned her that she could be facing trouble.

The speakers had stepped from behind the rear corner of the saloon and were only a short distance from the brunette. Tall, lean, dirty looking, they were shaggy haired and unshaven. Each wore a battered and grimy, formerly dark blue, Burnside campaign hat, a fringed buckskin shirt well coated with grease and dried blood, threadbare U.S. cavalry breeches in a no more cleanly condition and filthy Indian moccasins topped by matching knee length leggings from the same source. Although their gunbelts were of military manufacture, the tops had been removed from the high riding holsters at the right side and a hunting knife was suspended in its sheath on the left.

Studying the pair with a far greater knowledge than a newcomer from the East would have possessed, "Cornelia" deduced. they were buffalo hunters. What was more, the way each was swaying as they approached her supported the indications provided by their slurred tones that they were much the worse for drink. Even if she had retained the character of a "good" woman, she might not have escaped their attentions. Giving the appearance of being a girl of the area, she certainly would not.

To make matters worse, the brunette realized that the buffalo hunters had come upon her at a most inauspicious moment. If she had seen them earlier, she could have withdrawn from the alley and taken another route to her destination. As it was, should she turn and flee, they would be sure to give chase. She considered that this would be most inadvisable. A quick glance over her shoulder informed her that nobody was in sight on the street, but she had no desire to attract attention to herself by being pursued on to it. While somebody might come to her assistance in all probability, there was almost certain to be a disturbance which would bring peace officers upon the scene. Even as the wronged party, she might be subjected to a search and there were too many items which would demand explanation for her to want such a thing to happen.

"I just bet she kisses up a storm, Cousin Ezra!" declared the slightly shorter of the drunken twosome, leering at "Cornelia" in a way which confirmed her fears regarding their motives.

"Ain't but the one way to find out, Cousin Abednego," the second asserted, striding forward more rapidly than his kinsman and raising his hands.

If the completely passive way in which the brunette behaved as he was taking hold of her shoulders struck "Cousin Ezra" as strange, he apparently assumed she was too alarmed by what was happening to either try to oppose his attentions physically or scream for help.

The appearance of passivity proved to be *very* deceptive.

Although "Cornelia" had a deadly weapon in her reticule, she made no attempt to draw it. Instead, she allowed the buffalo hunter to pull her towards him without offering the slightest resistance. Allowing the reticule and jacket to slip from her grasp, she hitched up her skirt to permit a greater freedom of movement. On being brought to an appropriate distance, she put this to use in a most effective fashion.

Rising swiftly and with all the force the shapely, yet powerful muscles of the leg could supply, the brunette's right knee passed between her assailant's spread apart thighs. Caught in that portion of the masculine anatomy most susceptible to such an assault, the attack being delivered with a violence which split the knee of the black silk stocking covering her leg, he gave a strangled howl of what was intended to be a profane protest. However, it emerged as a garbled and unintelligible sound. Reeling away from his intended victim, he sent his hands to the stricken region and collapsed almost fainting through the agony.

Nor did "Cousin Abednego" fare any better!

Never the fastest of thinkers, liquor always had the effect

of dulling the second buffalo hunter's far from active perceptions. Before his restricted faculties could fully assimilate what had taken place, much less suggest how he could avenge the injury sustained by his cousin, he was prevented from doing either.

Allowing her skirt to fall, "Cornelia" pivoted rapidly and with an almost balletic grace. There was, however, nothing pacific about the rest of her movements. Swinging around with a precision many a man might have envied as the propellant force of her momentum was added to the impulsion of her far from fragile body, her clenched right fist shot out. The knuckles impacted against the lanky buffalo hunter's bristle-covered chin. His head snapped sideways and, pitching away from her in an uncontrollable spin, he struck the wall of the saloon. Rebounding from the unyielding timbers, he measured his length on the ground alongside his doubled up and moaning cousin. In his case, however, he lay without either sound or movement.

"Such behaviour to a lady, even one 'of easy virtue,' for shame!" the brunette said quietly, opening and shaking her right hand in an attempt to relieve the pain caused by delivering the blow. While her accent was still that of a Southron of good breeding and education, it was even crisper and more decisive than when she had been pretending to be annoyed with Kramer. "You-all just asked to be hurt, doing such an ungentlemanly thing. Not that either of you skin hunting son-of-bitches even starts to be a gentleman."

Having delivered the sentiment, "Cornelia" once again glanced around. Relieved to discover that the incident had gone unnoticed by anybody in the vicinity, she gathered up her belongings and walked by the two discomfited buffalo hunters without giving either so much as a glance. Her departure was unchallenged and, after strolling at a fast pace for a short while, she arrived at her destination.

Entering a small rooming house, the brunette waved a hand to the woman who looked out of the sitting-room and went upstairs without offering to explain her presence. Going to one of the rooms on the second floor, she delivered a knock which was clearly intended as a signal. The door was opened by the taller of the Indian-dark men who had provided the distraction in the alley outside the hotel. Nodding a greeting, she walked by him and found that, as she had anticipated, his companion and the "seller" of the jewels were also present.

"You took him like Grant took Richmond, Belle," praised the man who had introduced himself to Kramer as "Franz Schmidt" and, despite his assertion that he could only speak German, he employed English with only the slightest trace of an accent.

"*We* took him, Franz," the brunette corrected, suggesting at least one part of the identification he had given to *der Fleischer* was not an alias; just as the name he called her by would have supplied any peace officer who had chanced to hear it with a clue to the true identity of "Cornelia von Blücherdorf," allegedly of Atlanta, Georgia. "Although, as a Southron, I think you could have picked a better simile."

"I'm sorry, I wasn't thinking," the blond apologized with a smile, pleased by the way in which Belle Starr had so unhesitatingly shared the credit for the success of their undertaking. Then, noticing she was working the fingers of her right hand and massaging its knuckles with the left, he continued solicitously, "Have you hurt yourself?"

"Just a mite," the lady outlaw admitted, "I had a run in with a couple of skin hunters on the way here——And where do you pair think you're going?"

The question was elicited by the other two men exchanging glances, then starting to walk towards the door.

"Got sort of hot in here all of a sudden," the taller replied, with what might have been taken by some people as mildness. "Figured Sammy Crane and me'd go take a walk."

"It'll give us an appetite for supper, huh, Blue Duck?" the second man supplemented in an equally gentle manner.

"As you would say, Blue, in *three* words, 'For-get-*it*'!" Bell commanded, having been friendly with the pair for too many years to be misled by their apparently pacific demeanour. She was aware of what was implied by the use of the former's full name and the whole of the alias by which the other was always called. "Even if Mrs. Bentley downstairs deserved you having anything to *improve* your appetites, the last thing we need with what we've got ahead and the town being so peaceful right now, is for you two wild Cherokees going out looking for those jaspers so you can whittle their ears to sharp points. Besides which, I reckon they're sorry enough right now that they were ever taken with the notion."

"Damned if you're not getting to be a regular spoilsport since you stopped being a blonde," complained Sammy Crane, as he and his companion halted. "We haven't had no fun since we hit town. Have we, Blue?"

"Nary a smidgin," Blue Duck confirmed. "I'd head back home to the Nations and look for some, only they're laying for me down there."

"Here's the money, Belle," the blond remarked, having grown accustomed to the intense loyalty shown to the brunette by the two men and equally aware that neither would have accepted references to their birthright being part Cherokee Indian if uttered by anybody else. Taking the bulging wallet from the inside pocket of his jacket, he dropped it on to the dressing table and went on, "And you were right when you said we could take the chance of him not having noticed me at the women's boxing match last night."

"I felt sure he'd have been far too engrossed watching *them* to have paid any attention to the *men* who were there," Belle answered dryly, although she could have pointed out that the seller of the jewels had been dressed in a far more elegant fashion the previous evening and had neither spoken nor been close to their intended victim. "In fact, I'm surprised *you* noticed *him*."

"Who could miss him?" the blond snorted, but continued in a way which made it clear his attitude was created by thinking of the person they were discussing and not the brunette. "That big fat Westphalian *fleischer* stands out like a pig he's hung to butcher and sounds even worse."

"You're a snob, Franz," Belle said with a smile, guessing the outburst was caused by the way Kramer had treated her associate at the hotel. "But that's what makes you so convincing for the part you play."

If anybody else had made either of the comments to the blond, he would have taken offence.

As *der Fleischer* had suspected, the young man bore a more aristocratic and impressive name than "Schmidt." His name was, in fact, Franz Otto Ludwig von Lindeiner. Possessing a background almost identical with that ascribed to the non-existent Prussian who "Cornelia" had claimed was involved in the theft of the *Comtesse de* Saint-Pierre's collection of jewellery, the outlook with which he had been instilled made him far less tolerant as a rule. However, since meeting and starting to work with Belle Starr, he had developed a far higher opinion of her than he would previously have believed was possible where a woman was concerned. Such was the esteem in which he held her that, even if he had not known the two men were waiting for him close by, he would never have even thought of absconding with the proceeds of the "diamond switch" confidence trick as might have been the case if he was working with an all male "team."

Nor was von Lindeiner's respect for the brunette caused by having had a sexual relationship with her. This had not been the case. When he had hinted at the possibility early in their association, she had given a definite refusal. Yet it had been done in such a manner that neither his feelings nor ego had been hurt.

"I thought you'd find some way of calling it off when those two men of his came on the scene," the blond remarked. "Then I could see he'd set your back hair to rising by the way he was behaving towards you and knew you'd go ahead. But I don't mind admitting I was far from easy in my mind, knowing they were waiting outside and us with no other way of leaving unless we jumped from one of the windows."

"I could see you were worried," Belle admitted, but with no suggestion of reproof. "It gave you just that kind of anxiety that made you all the more convincing. For all that, I won't be sorry if there's no cause for worry with Mr. Glemnitz."

"*Glemnitz*?" von Lindeiner repeated, omitting the honorific. There was an intonation in his voice that suggested he had mixed emotions about the name. "Do you think it's safe for us to go after him now we've taken *der Fleischer*?"

Gustav Glemnitz was the name of the original victim selected by the lady outlaw. However, having learned that Kramer was a wealthy dealer in cattle and formed what that proved to be an accurate summation of his character, she had elected to take advantage of Glemnitz's absence from Ellsworth on business by making him the target for the "diamond switch" confidence trick.

"Why not?" Belle answered confidently. "We've still got enough fake stones and duplicate pouches to take two more suckers." Having crossed to sit at the dressing-table and place her reticule upon it while the conversation was taking place, she indicated the blond's wallet and went on, "We've made nine thousand out of Kramer, Franz, and Glemnitz should be good for almost as much."

"*Nine* thousand?" von Lindeiner questioned, just a trifle suspiciously, knowing how much money was in the wallet and aware that there had been occasions when stating there was more loot than there actually was provided an excuse for cutting out the member of the team who had had it in his possession.

"Of course," Belle confirmed, guessing what had provoked the reaction from the blond, but showing no animosity. Opening the reticule, she took out the money it held, "Did you forget that Kramer paid me a 'commission' of five hundred dollars for my 'services'?"

"But what if *der Fleischer* sees us with Glemnitz?" von Lindeiner asked, deciding that all he had been told about Belle Starr's reputation for fair dealing with her associates was correct and feeling a change of subject was advisable. If she had chosen to disclaim the payment of the "commission," the other two men would have accepted her word without question and, tough as he was personally, he did not care to contemplate the consequences of having them believe he was cheating them of five hundred dollars. "I know he's not smart, but even *he* will guess something's wrong."

"He would, *if* he was around to see us," Belle conceded, aware of what was worrying the blond. However, having been certain that the confidence trick could be carried out just as successfully with the original victim, she had taken steps to learn whether it would be safe for them to go ahead. "I'm not meeting Glemnitz until tomorrow morning and Kramer will be gone by that time."

"Can we be sure he's *going*?" von Lindeiner wanted to know. "It's not that I'm doubting you, Belle, but——!"

"I know," the brunette interrupted. "I'd rather be sure than sorry too, and I'm as sure as I can be. After you left, I gave him a hint that there could be something more to come than just *dinner* if he took me to eat tonight. At the risk of seeming immodest, I'm sure he'd have taken me up on it if he hadn't been leaving on the east-bound train this afternoon."

"This afternoon, huh?" von Lindeiner said. Showing a

mixture of relief and satisfaction, he continued, "Then he *hasn't* heard about the fight tonight."

"What fight would that be?" Belle queried. "Don't tell me it's those women boxers again?"

"Not *boxers*," the blond corrected, grinning. "Barney Maters at the Longhorn Saloon's got two of the girls to put on a knockdown, drag-out hair-yanking fight tonight. I thought I'd have to miss it because *der Fleischer* would be sure to be there, which would have annoyed Joy seeing that I helped arrange it. But he won't be in town, so I'll be able to go."

"The way you men spend your time!" Belle sniffed, but with more amusement than disapproval or criticism in her tone. Then she swung her gaze to the two Indian-dark silent men and said, "We'll take Glemnitz in the morning. But, just to be on the safe side, you'd best go to the depot and make sure Kramer does leave."

"Here he is," Blue Duck drawled, as the east-bound train came to a halt, looking to where Ernst Kramer and his two bodyguards, the latter carrying all the party's baggage between them, had appeared at the other end of the railroad depot. "I thought the son-of-a——!"

"Hell's fires!" Sammy Crane interrupted, stiffening and speaking in what was—for one of his generally unemotional nature—considerable alarm and urgency. "Look at who-all's coming off the train!"

"Hot damn, yes!" the taller of Belle Starr's part-Cherokee associates ejaculated, displaying a similar consternation—although usually just as little prone to letting his feelings show —as he turned his attention in the required direction. "It's *Jubal Framant*, as I live and breathe. Which likely wouldn't be for *long* had he seen us *first*."

Having halted on the platform of the leading passenger car, oblivious to the fact that he was preventing a man and women behind him from leaving the train, the cause of their comments was studying the people gathered outside the depot. His gaze ran from one to another of them in a fashion similar to that of a rancher inspecting livestock to decide whether any would be worth buying, or a butcher selecting animals to be killed.

Being aware that Jubal Framant was a bounty hunter and

hired killer, if they had given the matter any thought, Blue Duck and Sammy Crane would have considered the latter description more apt. However, at that moment, they were concerned solely with keeping out of his sight. They were relieved that on their arrival they had taken the precaution of selecting a position from which they could watch the passengers boarding without their own presence being noticeable, even though this had been instinctive rather than through any belief they had need to do so.

Just over six foot in height and in his late forties, Framant was scrawny rather than hefty in build. There was a suggestion of arrogance about his cadaverous features, but also something which hinted he considered he could handle any objections taken to his person in spite of his far from imposing physique. A tan coloured J.B. Stetson hat with a "Montana Peak" crown[1] sat on the back of his head of close-cropped darkish hair. He had on a crumpled, expensive brown three-piece suit, the trousers ending in the legs of unpolished black riding boots, and his grubby shirt had no collar. Around his waist was a well made gunbelt, with two revolvers—the butts of which were of a shape that implied they were not the products of Colt's Patent Firearms Manufacturing Company of Hartford, Connecticut, or of any other maker in the United States of America—in holsters seemingly too long to permit their rapid withdrawal. Nor were they his only weapons. The twin barrels of the ten gauge shotgun he was carrying rested on his right shoulder and the watchers did not believe its sole purpose was to serve as a counter balance for the carpetbag in his left hand.

"What the hell's brought him here, Blue?" Sammy Crane asked, as the bounty hunter completed the scrutiny without having seen them, then descended from the platform.

"I dunno," Blue Duck admitted. "Come on. Kramer's hauling his butt back to home, but Belle might not want to go after Glemnitz seeing's how the bounty hunting son-of-a-bitch's in town."

"I'm betting she does take him, like she said," Sammy Crane asserted. "That gal never could, nor would back off

---

1. *"Montana peak" crown: a way of shaping a hat so it resembled the headdress which was formerly worn by boy scouts. J.T.E.*

from *anything* once she's set her mind down to doing it, safe or not."

Retiring from their place of concealment, the two men walked away. If they had stayed only a few seconds longer, they would have been less confident that they had carried out the duty to which they were assigned by the lady outlaw.

CHAPTER FIVE

I Won't Be Leaving Until Tomorrow

"Hey, boss!" called a voice which Ernst Kramer had no doubt was addressing him. It made him pause instead of going aboard after those passengers had disembarked whose journey on the east-bound train was terminated at Ellsworth. "Hold hard there, this's important!"

Turning, *der Fleischer* confirmed his assumption that he was the person being asked to wait. The man who had attracted his attention was one of his agents and, in fact, the most important of those who took care of his primary business interests throughout the north-western States.

In spite of wearing clothing suggesting he was connected with the hauling of freight by wagons to points west of the Mississippi River where the railroad did not reach, Jebediah Lincoln's massive frame was far more corpulent than was usually the lot of those who performed the actual tasks in that hard-worked industry. Such was his haste that his Burnside campaign hat had fallen off, but was retained on his shoulders by its *barbiquejo* chinstrap, which exposed a balding thatch of light brown hair rendered almost black by a liberal application of bay rum.[1] His sun reddened features would have been jovial if it had not been for his small and close set eyes. At that moment, he was even more flushed and glistening with the perspiration accrued by his having hurried to the depot bearing

1. *"Bay rum": an aromatic liquid obtained at that period by distilling rum with the leaves of the bayberry tree,* Pimenta racemosa, *used as a medicine and a cosmetic, in the latter case chiefly as a hair dressing for men. J.T.E.*

44

information he felt certain would be of great interest to his employer.[2]

Lincoln wore a fancily stitched, fringed buckskin jacket, an open necked tartan shirt that clashed badly with his multi-coloured bandana, yellowish-brown Nankeen trousers and blunt toed, flat heeled riding boots, none of which showed signs of having ever been subjected to hard use. Nor did the coiled bull whip he carried with its handle thrust through a leather loop on the left side of his waist belt. This and the garments were merely an affectation intended to impress people. Although he had no weapons in plain sight, the revolver in its shoulder holster was betrayed by a bulge on the left side of the jacket.

"Well?" Kramer demanded, never the most polite of men when dealing with those he considered to be his social inferiors.

"I thought you couldn't have heard about it, boss," Lincoln claimed, somewhat breathlessly and holding his voice down to lower than its usual booming level. "But there's going to be a fight between two saloon girls tonight."

"Is there, by god?" *der Fleischer* ejaculated, eagerness replacing the irritation he had been showing and he paid no attention to the call of, "All aboard!" being given by the train's conductor. *"Where and when?"*

"They're having it at a barn outside town at half past eight," Lincoln explained, being aware of his employer's predilection for watching women fighting and gratified by the favourable response to the news he had brought.[3] "I've only

---

2. *The exact nature of the duties carried out by Jebediah Lincoln on the behalf of Ernst "der Fleischer" Kramer are described in:* THE WHIP AND THE WAR LANCE. *J.T.E.*

3. *How the life of Ernst "der Fleischer" Kramer was affected by his predilection is told in:* Part Five, Belle "the Rebel Spy" Boyd in "The Butcher's Fiery End," J.T.'S LADIES. *Information regarding others who found a similar pleasure in watching women fighting—Albert Brickhouse in Juarez, Mexico and the members of the Pinhole Club, Leicester Place, London, England, during the 1920's and, more recently, "Hippolyta" and Oscar Burgenhof, who resided in Gusher City, Texas, until their careers were ended by Woman Deputy Alice Fayde and Deputy Sheriff Bradford Counter of the Rockabye County Sheriff's Office—can be found chronologically in:* RAPIDO CLINT: "CAP" FOG, TEXAS RANGER, MEET MR. J. G. REEDER *and* BAD HOMBRE. *J.T.E.*

just now got word about it myself, but I've managed to get us in as———!''

"Hey, mister!" the conductor called impatiently, walking up and causing the corpulent freighter to stop speaking. "Are you getting aboard, or staying here?"

"I'm *staying!*" Kramer stated, without a moment's hesitation, the Germanic timbre in his voice growing more pronounced as he contemplated the reason for his decision to postpone the journey. After the railroad official had gone away, he turned and addressed the two burly young men holding the baggage. "Take that back to the hotel and get me the suite, if it's still vacant, or a room of any kind." Then he glanced at his other employee and went on, "I'll send a telegraph message to let them know at home I won't be leaving until tomorrow."

"See how fast you can strip her raw, Jill!"

"Let's have her peeled naked as a jaybird, Joy!"

Such were the instructions being delivered vociferously by the all-male audience, along with variations on the same theme, as Ernst Kramer and Jebediah Lincoln somewhat belatedly made their way to the seats which the latter had procured for them at a high price (which Kramer had not offered to refund.) The various suggestions were for the edification of the two young women who, having been introduced by the owner of the Longhorn Saloon as "Joy Turner" and "Jill Hambling," were moving towards each other in a confidently determined fashion across the roped-off open space at the centre of the big barn some five miles south of Ellsworth, Kansas.

Der Fleischer had found the suite of rooms in the Columbus Grand Hotel which he had occupied earlier were still vacant, but he considered that he had been less fortunate where another matter was concerned. On inquiring after "Cornelia von Blücherdorf," his knocks on her door having elicited no response, he was informed by the desk clerk that she had left earlier and had not yet returned. Remembering she had said she would be busy until that evening, he had seen nothing suspicious in the news. He was writing a note inviting her to take dinner with him after the fight, without mentioning the reason for his absence until the appointed time, when a business associate had chanced to see him and asked if they could discuss a deal of some magnitude. Always willing to turn a profit, particularly as its accomplishment would not interfere with his attending the fight and the later hoped-for dalliance with the brunette, he had agreed. Finishing the note and leaving it with the clerk, he had taken the man to his rooms. The meal he had had sent up and the protracted session of bargaining had caused him to be later than he anticipated before setting out for the first part of the evening's entertainment. Learning in passing that "Cornelia" still had not put in an appearance, he had repeated his instructions to the clerk.

While riding to the barn in the fringe-topped surrey hired by Lincoln (also without any suggestion of the cost being reimbursed), Kramer had discovered why the need to select such an out of the way location had arisen. Due to having been subjected to considerable pressure by the members of the Ladies For The Betterment of Ellsworth Society—who had already protested vigorously about the women's boxing matches, although unsuccessful in their bid to have the programme cancelled—the town marshal had stated he would not allow the all-in-fight between the girls to take place in the Longhorn Saloon. However, he was equally desirous of avoiding antagonizing the influential male citizens who wished to see it, and he had pointed out in private to the owner that he would have no legal right to intervene should the combatants settle their differences outside his "bailiwick." The barn, which had been donated by an enthusiastic wealthy local businessman for the occasion, stood some distance beyond the recognized boundary of the town and did not come under his jurisdiction.

According to Lincoln, in spite of the solution offered by the marshal, it had not been considered advisable to publicise the event too openly. To have done so could have led to the "good" women of the town seeking to involve the sheriff of Ellsworth County, whose jurisdiction extended beyond the city limits and included the area in which the barn was situated. For all that, sufficient "word of mouth" advertising had ensured a good attendance in spite of the high price which the owner of the saloon had claimed was necessary as a result of his added expenses.

Having heard the names of the combatants being announced as he was dismounting from the surrey, *der Fleischer* had been too afraid of missing anything to walk to the front of the building. Instead, he and his two employees had entered through the side door. The reduction in the size of his entourage had been due to the bank being closed by the time he had returned from the railroad depot. Being unable to deposit his cash box there for safekeeping and disinclined to take chances where it was concerned, he had left one of the burly young men at the hotel with orders to remain in the suite and guard it. The other had driven them to the barn, but did not receive the full benefit of Lincoln's largesse. He was not allowed to sit with his employer and the freighter, but had to remain standing at the rear of the crowd near to where they had come in.

"I'm sorry I couldn't get us any closer, boss," Lincoln apologized, as he and Kramer were sitting down on the third row of extemporized seats made from bales of hay stacked in three steps.

"That's all right," *der Fleischer* replied, gazing downwards over the heads of the men occupying the two rows in front of him. "I can see everything."

Which was, although Kramer did not know it, much truer than he realized!

If *der Fleischer* had been less absorbed in looking at the roped-off area of the barn's floor, he might have noticed something familiar about the close-cropped blond head of the man in the front row who was sitting next to the owner of the Longhorn Saloon. However, in exculpation, even if he had seen the man, the attire of a successful professional gambler might have served to prevent him making an identification.

Oblivious to the proximity of a member of the "team" which had swindled him with the "diamond switch" confidence trick, Kramer ran the tip of his tongue over his lips and studied the combatants. They were circling one another warily, each apparently seeking an opening and with their hands held ready to grapple whenever there was an opportunity. Although neither came up to his Teutonic preference for tall and statuesque women, he had to admit they made an attractive sight.

Joy Turner was the younger, slightly shorter, but—as she was full breasted and curvaceously buxom—at no great disadvantage where weight was concerned. Reddish-brown hair was piled on her head and she was good looking, if just a trifle sharp featured. Despite being less well developed than her opponent, Jill Hambling was far from skinny and had a good figure. Her black hair was hanging loose in a way which emphasised the somewhat gypsyish look of her swarthily pretty face. They wore the usual knee-length and sleeveless dresses of saloongirls and black stockings, but had on neither jewellery nor shoes.

Having had considerable experience in staging similar events, *der Fleischer* could see that Barney Maters had taken precautions to prevent the girls inflicting permanently disfiguring damage upon one another. Not only would the absence of footwear reduce the force with which kicks could be delivered, but they were not wearing rings and their fingernails were trimmed until useless for scratching. Furthermore, if the way their feet sank into it was any guide, the surface of the roped-off area was covered by a tarpaulin which had been laid over a layer of straw. Kramer approved of this having been done. Once, when he had hired a couple of prostitutes to provide a similar entertainment at his mansion in Chicago, a fall to the unpadded floor of the dining-room had stunned both and ended what should have been a lengthy fight.

"Come on, damn it!" a voice shouted impatiently, bringing *der Fleischer's* train of speculation to an end. "Get to fighting instead of just walking around that way!"

As the cry was taken up with variations by other speculators, the girls lunged inwards. However, what happened next brought a grunt of disapproval from Kramer. Instead of grabbing for hair as was usually the case when members of their sex fought, each caught the other's left wrist in her right hand. With the holds obtained, they pushed and shoved for several seconds in what appeared to be a trial of strength.

Although the rest of the audience began to yell approval and encouragement, *der Fleischer* was less impressed by what he was seeing. He noticed that, despite each being presented with more than one opportunity as they surged together, neither offered to jerk up a leg and use the knee as a means of breaking what was close to a deadlock. Nor did he consider there was much improvement when they fell to the floor and started rolling over and over. While this displayed their fancy garters and the white flesh between the tops of the stockings and the hems of daringly short lace trimmed panties, their struggling was devoid of the kind of violence seen during a spontaneous conflict in less formal conditions.

"This's good, huh, boss?" Lincoln asked, sharing the other onlookers' appreciation of the sight as he watched Jill—whose torso was being straddled by Joy's plump thighs—tear open the side of the other's glossy green dress.

"Is it?" Kramer sniffed, feeling sure that the garment had already had a hole in it through which the older girl could insert her fingers and produce the damage. "I'd like to see either of them up against that maid of mine, Gretchen."

The comment went unnoticed by the freighter as, their positions having been reversed without any noticeable difficulty in Kramer's opinion, the red-head contrived to rip Jill's scarlet frock from hem to neckline. If any of the other spectators sharing *der Fleischer's* assumption that this was achieved by the provision of a similar aid, it was allowed to pass without protest. Instead, all of the audience—Kramer included—were treated to the not unenjoyable discovery that neither girl was wearing anything from the waist up beneath the outer garments.

Expending considerable vigour, Joy and Jill continued struggling for almost two minutes without a pause. Having spent some of the time rolling on the floor, they returned to their feet to do more scuffling and pushing until their unscientific wrestling took them down again. Although their clutching hands added to the demolition of the dresses and stockings, no slaps or punches were landed and, when hair was grabbed, neither applied her full strength to the pulling.

Attractively sensual as the majority of the onlookers were clearly finding the sight of the tussling girls, particularly with the bodices of the dresses trailing to leave each bare to the waist, nothing Kramer had seen happening was leading him to believe he was witnessing a genuine fight. For all that, as he watched them, he grudgingly conceded that they were giving as good a show of its kind as he had ever attended. Certainly neither was allowing it to become too obvious that they were merely simulating conflict. They had sufficient histrionic skill and physical agility to make their efforts appear fairly convincing.

Taking the latter point and the energy being expended by

both girls into consideration, *der Fleischer* was enjoying himself despite his misgivings. In fact, as he watched the fight, he was hoping for an improvement in the standard of the action. Based on experiences gained from other exhibitions of a similar nature he had attended, he knew there was something the owner of the Longhorn Saloon and the girls themselves might not have taken into account when deciding to make money by putting on a fake fight.

Twice the contingency envisaged by Kramer seemed about to happen, but did not as the girl who had inadvertently been hurt managed to hold her temper in check and avoided making an equally painful retaliation.

Then the situation for which *der Fleischer* was hoping occurred!

"Bite her on the apples, Jill-gal!" whooped an excited spectator. "That'll make her let go of you!"

Somehow during the course of their tussling on the floor, the older girl had come to be lying behind Joy and trapped in a headlock. It was applied with such vigour that her face was being pressed against the red head's bare and imposing bosom and because the arm around her throat was pressing so tightly she could not complain about the pain inflicted by the hold. Whether she acted upon the spectator's advice, or of her own accord, the result was the same. Opening her mouth, she gave the breast a sharp nip. A yelp of pain, the first to have been uttered by either combatant, burst from Joy and, while the bite achieved the promised result, Jill's liberation proved far from being a blessing.

Opening her arms, Joy clenched and jerked up her right fist before the older girl's head could be withdrawn. Instinctive though the action was, the knuckles caught Jill on the nose with sufficient force to elicit a squeak of pain-filled protest and it provoked an instant reprisal. Flying up with pain from the blow, her fingers sank into the red head's back hair. This time, there was no restraint in the way she began to pull. Nor was there in Joy's response to the suffering being inflicted upon her.

Feeling herself being dragged down, the red head employed the kind of agility she had exhibited earlier—if less effectively—by rolling backwards over her assailant. Although her action caused her hair to be released, the resultant pain led to further aggression. Alighting on her knees, she grabbed Jill's left breast with her right hand and, as she started to squeeze, the fingers of her left ploughed deeply into the black hair to tug at it with a vigour not previously employed. Yelping furiously, the older girl twisted her torso free from the clutching grasp. Sitting up, she lashed around a slap which left a red mark on Joy's cheek and ended any chance of a return to their earlier play-acting.

As *der Fleischer* had seen happen on other occasions when girls were simulating a fight and a chance injury caused a loss of temper, all pretence was ended and the real thing erupted.

Nor was Kramer alone in realizing what was taking place!

Watching Joy return the slap with one equally hard and the way in which both girls set about pulling hair in earnest, Franz von Lindeiner became aware things were not going as planned. To give him credit, despite one of the organizers of what had proved to be a lucrative form of entertainment, he had no desire to see either Jill or Joy hurt more than was necessary. Twisting around to see what the owner of the Longhorn Saloon was going to do, and deciding that the answer was nothing, he started to rise. Catching him by the arm and hauling him down, Maters warned that any attempt to separate the combatants would be resisted strenuously by the spectators as they had been promised a fight to a finish.

Despite Kramer having been presented with a view of the blond's face, even if only briefly, the full significance of the sight failed to make any impression upon him at that moment. Although it registered subconsciously, he was too engrossed in the changed state of affairs within the roped-off area to pay any attention to the nagging thought that he had seen something of importance.

Struggling to their feet and carrying on with their efforts, the girls gave *der Fleischer* no further cause for complaint. While there was nothing scientific about their methods, they went at each other with serious intent. Such was the ferocity with which they assailed each other that they had cause to be grateful for the precautions taken to avoid them sustaining injuries which would have left them permanently scarred. While they had not done so previously, they now showed no hesitation over delivering slaps, punches and kicks. However, the lack of nails and rings lessened the damage they were capable of inflicting. For all that, by the time they grappled and tripped to crash to the floor, Joy's nose was bleeding and Jill's top lip was cut.

Encouraged by the spectators, although neither was conscious of it, the fight raged for almost five minutes. That it remained within the confines of the roped-off area was by chance rather than through deliberate intent. The rehearsing the girls had done was forgotten. All either could think of was how to repay the punishment being inflicted upon her and even this was mostly accomplished instinctively, with neither gaining any noticeable advantage. The result was still anything but certain when, clad only in their now tattered panties and ruined stockings, they returned to their feet once more after the third gruelling mill across the floor.

For the first time since they had begun to fight in earnest, the girls went into the kind of trial of strength with which they had commenced their efforts. On this occasion, Jill brought her knee into play. Fortunately for Joy, exhaustion caused the attack to be delivered with less force than would have been the case earlier. Even at the reduced power, it caused her to give a croaking gasp. Snatching her hands free and doubling over, she threw her arms around the other girl's thighs. Hugging tightly in an instinctive action intended to save her from similar punishment, she sank to her knees. The attempt was only partially successful.

While Jill was prevented from using her knee, both hands were free. Grasping the now tangled and dishevelled red hair with the left, she began to land hard slaps to Joy's bare shoulders and back with the right. The pain she was causing drove the younger girl to a desperate response. Letting go of the legs and forcing herself upwards, she thrust with her arms. Her palms landed on Jill's already sore bosom hard enough to achieve her purpose.

Releasing the red head's hair, the older girl stumbled back a few steps. Bracing herself on spread apart feet, Joy swung a punch as Jill was returning the attack. Wildly as it was delivered and her exhaustion notwithstanding, it proved effective. Walking straight into it, Jill went over and landed supine. Collapsing rather than sinking to sit astride her stomach, oblivious of the fact that she was incapable of resistance, the red head took her by the throat with both hands and weakly began to bang her head on the floor.

"Well, it's over now, Dutchy," Maters said to von Lindeiner. "But you'd best go stop that girl of yours, she doesn't seem to know it."

CHAPTER SIX

We've Come for the Jewels

"Good evening, Miss von Blücherdorf," greeted the desk clerk on duty at the Columbus Grand Hotel, looking up from his study of the register as he became aware that somebody was approaching. "We've had the broken pane in your window replaced."

"I'm pleased to hear it," Belle Starr replied, having intended to inquire whether the repair had been carried out.

"This telegraph message has just arrived," the clerk went on, turning and reaching towards the appropriate pigeonhole in the mail rack, before the brunette could walk away. "And Mr. Kramer left this note for you when he went out."

"Mr. *Kramer*?" Belle repeated, managing to show none of her surprise and consternation by the latter piece of information, as she accepted the buff coloured envelope containing the telegraph message and the sheet of folded paper which were being offered to her by the man behind the desk. "I thought he'd left."

"He checked out earlier," the clerk admitted, glancing at the register. "But he came back again and took his suite for the night."

"I thought it was only we women who changed our minds," Belle said pensively, opening the sheet of paper.

On being informed by Blue Duck and Sammy Crane of Jubal Framant's arrival, the brunette had considered it was unlikely that he was looking for them. There was no bounty offered for any of them, or for Franz von Lindeiner, to cause them to be the object of his attentions. However, in accordance with her policy of "better sure than sorry," she had stated her intention of trying to find out why he was visiting

Ellsworth. The decision had caused her to delay returning to
the hotel and discovering that *der Fleischer* had postponed his
departure.

She had waited until the early evening before she left to
satisfy her curiosity. She had spent the time changing her appearance in the room she rented at the house her "team" were
using as their headquarters. Wearing a wig of fiery red hair,
suitable make-up and more garish clothes than those in which
she had arrived, she had been sure that nobody would recognize her while she was carrying out her investigation.

In every town of any size, even one of such recent and
rapid growth as Ellsworth, there were sources of information
available to members of the criminal element. Seeking out a
man who fell into that category, Belle had been told enough to
make her feel sure she was correct in her assumption with
regards to the arrival of the bounty hunter. Further confirmation had come when she heard he had killed a wanted outlaw
for whom he had clearly been waiting in a saloon.

Returning to the rooming house, the brunette had told Blue
Duck and Sammy Crane the result of her inquiries. Although
von Lindeiner had already left for the barn, being unaware
that Kramer had learned the fight was to take place, she had
felt no concern. Reverting to her former attire and appearance,
she had returned to the hotel accompanied by the two men.
They were waiting in the alley to receive instructions for the
distraction they were to provide should the "diamond switch"
confidence trick be played the following day.

"I hope it's not bad news, Miss von Blücherdorf," the clerk
said solicitously, after the lady outlaw had finished reading
both messages.

"Not really," Belle lied and held out *der Fleischer's* note.
"Will you put this back where it came from please and, if Mr.
Kramer asks after me, tell him I still haven't come back."

"Of course, Miss von Blücherdorf," the clerk assented,
concluding correctly that the brunette had no wish to accept
the other guest's invitation, although her motives were different from those he suspected.

Turning from the desk after glancing at the clock on the
wall, Belle went into the dining-room. Instead of taking a seat
at one of the tables, she passed straight through and left by the
side entrance.

"You can forget Glemnitz," the brunette informed her waiting companions. "He's sent a telegraph message saying he won't be back here for a couple of days—and Kramer's come back."

"He looked like he was fixing to get on the train when we pulled out," Sammy Crane protested. "Has he found out we took him?"

"No," Belle stated with assurance. "But I think, from the time he asked me to have dinner with him, that he heard about the fight between those two girls. You'd better go out there and see what's happening, Blue."

"Hell, yes!" Blue Duck agreed. "The Dutchman's[1] there and, if Kramer sees him, all hell's going to pop."

"Or it's already popped," Crane went on.

"We'd best find out, either way," Belle declared. "Wait here, Sammy. I'll go and pack my gear, then—hey, though. If he didn't go on the train, that cash box of his will be in his room. The bank would be closed, so he couldn't have left it there."

"I hope you're not figuring on doing what I *know* you're figuring on doing!" Blue Duck growled.

"I am," Belle admitted. "Get going, Blue and you stay put, Sammy. It won't take me very long."

Such was the confidence each of the men felt in the lady outlaw's judgement and ability that neither raised any objections to her decision. Exchanging a glance redolent of amused admiration with Crane as she returned to the dining-room, Blue Duck set off to carry out her instructions.

Despite the quickness with which she had decided to commit the robbery, Belle was not acting on impulse alone. She was gambling upon having sufficient time to carry out her intentions and escape before Kramer returned to the hotel. A shrewd judge of human nature, as anyone leading a "team" of confidence tricksters must be, she felt sure that a man who was so eager to watch two women fighting that he postponed his plans to go home at the last moment would be unlikely to pay too much attention to his surroundings on arriving at the scene of the conflict. Unless they were brought into close

---

1. *"Dutchman:" in the West, members of the Teutonic races were frequently referred to as being Dutch even if they did not come from the Netherlands. J.T.E.*

contact, he might not notice von Lindeiner. Or he might not recognize "Schmidt" if they met as the blond would be dressed in a different fashion and was able to speak English instead of being restricted to German.

Nor had the brunette discounted the possibility of there being somebody in *der Fleischer's* suite. She did not doubt that at least one of his bodyguards would have been left behind to keep watch over the contents of his cash box. In fact, this was the main reason she believed the scheme she was contemplating would be workable. There was a small vial in her reticule which would enable her to cope with whoever was in the room provided she could persuade him, or them, to take a drink.

Once again, Belle did not sit down in the dining-room. Asking the waitress to fetch her a bottle of brandy, she took it with her when it was delivered and went upstairs. There was nobody in sight as she knocked on the door of *der Fleischer's* suite which was opened by the burly young man who had collected the cash box from the bank so that the "jewels" could be purchased.

"Good evening," Belle greeted. "Is Mr. Kramer here?"

"Not yet," the young man replied.

"His note said for me to come up and wait for him," Belle claimed, watching for any indication that the bodyguard knew this to be untrue, or that he had his companion with him.

"Come in then," the man offered without hesitation, remembering the comments made by his employer about the visitor and having no doubt that such an invitation had been given to her.

"Are you alone?" Belle inquired glancing around the sitting-room as she entered and the door was closed behind her.

"Yes," the young man admitted, making no attempt to conceal his annoyance over having been given the boring duty.

"Will Mr. Kramer be long?" the brunette went on, pleased by the information and the tone in which it was delivered.

"I shouldn't think so," the man answered. "He didn't say what time he'd be back."

"Oh well, I've nothing else to do so I may as well wait for him," Belle declared, crossing to the table and, placing the bottle on it, she drew out a chair to sit down. "I do so feel like a drink, but it isn't lady-like to drink alone. Perhaps you will join me, sir?"

"I wouldn't say 'no,'" the man asserted, studying the visitor in a speculative fashion and drawing the conclusions that Belle had hoped he would. "I'll get glasses from his bedroom."

While the bodyguard was doing as he had promised, the brunette worked swiftly. She had loosened the cork of the bottle on her way upstairs and removed it. Then, taking the vial from her reticule, she extracted its stopper and kept it concealed in her left hand.

"Oh, dear," Belle gasped, after her impromptu host had come back with two glasses and poured a generous amount of the brandy into each. "I'm not a big, strong man like you-all. So I can't drink this as it is. Could you fetch me some water to have in it, please?"

"Sure," the bodyguard replied.

Reaching across the table as soon as the man's back was turned, the brunette tipped some of the vial's contents into his glass. Then, as he disappeared into Kramer's bedroom again, she shook the glass to mix the two liquids. Having done so, she replaced the vial's stopper. Once more, she acted with sufficient speed to prevent him from discovering anything untowards had taken place when he returned carrying the carafe from his employer's washstand.

"Your health, sir," Belle said, raising her glass after having diluted its contents and without offering the carafe for the bodyguard to do the same.

"And yours," the man responded, remembering the comment about his masculinity and refraining from adding water to his brandy.

"Mercy me!" Belle gasped in well simulated admiration, watching the bodyguard taking an appreciative gulp of the liquor instead of sipping as she had done. "I wish I could take it like that."

"This French stuff's *nothing*!" the man claimed. "You should try schnapps. Now there's a *real* drink for you."

"I'm sure it is," Belle replied. "But I doubt whether we could get any here. Finish that and have another."

"Thanks," the man answered, disposing of the remaining brandy with a single swallow.

However, before the invitation could be accepted, the drug took effect. As Belle reached for the glass she was being offered, it slipped from the bodyguard's fingers. Although he began to realize what was happening when he felt the wave of dizziness assailing him, there was nothing he could do to counteract it. Commencing what should have been a profane threat in German, he tried to rise. The words went uncompleted and the attempt was to no avail. His legs buckled beneath him and, despite a brief resistance to try and remain erect, he slid helplessly to the floor

"Well now," Belle remarked with a smile, coming to her feet and stepping around the table. "This 'French stuff' was a whole heap more potent than you-all imagined. I'd hate to have *your* head in the morning, apart from what your boss is likely to do to you."

As she spoke she removed her victim's collar and tie, then opened the neck of his shirt. Then she went into the main bedroom. Testing the door of the wardrobe, she found it was fastened and the key had been removed. However, she was prepared for such a contingency. Taking a small tool shaped like a later generation's "iron" golf club from her reticule, it served just as well when inserted into the hole and manipulated. It proved equally efficacious on the lock of the small leather portmaneau in which she found what she had come to steal.

Taking the cash box to the bed, Belle had just as little difficulty in opening it. Helping herself to the money, she tucked it into her capacious reticule alongside the holster of the modified Manhattan Navy revolver which she had refrained from drawing when accosted by the two buffalo hunters.[2] Her first thought was to leave the buckskin pouch containing the false jewels, but she changed her mind and removed it. However, having no desire to further crowd the reticule—as this would make the weapon noticeable and reduce the speed at which it could be drawn in an emergency she did not place the bag in her reticule with the money.

Having achieved her purpose, the brunette decided it was

2. *The nature of the modifications and further information regarding the Manhattan Navy revolver are given in:* Footnote 4, CHAPTER SEVEN. *J.T.E.*

no use trying to conceal traces of her activities. The discovery of the unconscious guard would warn Kramer that something was amiss and immediately he was certain to guess what had happened. Leaving the open box on the bed, she was on the point of taking her departure when she noticed some of the stationery, a pen and a bottle of ink supplied by the hotel on the sidepiece. Remembering his attitude throughout the negotiations, she yielded to the impulse which assailed her. Going to the sidepiece she wrote a message on the top sheet of paper which would leave him in no doubt who was responsible for the robbery, but which might prevent him from suspecting the truth. With that done, she returned to the sitting-room carrying the reticule and pouch in her left hand. Checking that the passage was still deserted, she removed the key and left the suite. Locking the door, she tossed the key into the shadows before making for her own room.

Unfastening and opening the door, the lady outlaw saw nothing out of the ordinary in the lamp being lit. This was done every evening by the hotel's staff if the occupant was absent. However, on entering, she received a shock!

It was all too apparent that the room had been thoroughly searched!

Belle was not kept in ignorance of who were the culprits for very long!

Such was the shock of the discovery that the brunette moved forward involuntarily. She was almost in the centre of the room before her instincts began to warn her that she was acting in a most ill-advised fashion. Confirmation of her fears came from another source almost at once. Hearing the door being closed behind her, she swung around.

The sight which met Belle's gaze caused her to refrain from reaching into the reticule for her revolver and froze her into immobility.

Two men were standing on the hinged side of the door, having gone there on hearing the key being placed in the lock. They were concealed by the door when the lady outlaw entered with less than her usual caution. Their derby hats and suits were of eastern style and as costly as might be expected of guests in the Columbus Grand Hotel, which would allow them to avoid attracting unwanted attention if they should be seen there, but they had on western riding boots and their faces were deeply bronzed.

Despite noticing the discrepancy in their attire, at that moment, Belle was more concerned by the Colt 1860 Army revolver each of the visitors was pointing at her!

"Howdy, ma'am," the taller of the pair greeted, his accent indicating he had not been born and raised east of the Mississippi River no matter how he might be dressed. "We've come for the jewels."

Leaving his seat and paying no attention to the delighted response of the crowd, Franze von Lindeiner stepped over the rope. Quickly, crossing the padded tarpaulin, he circled around the girls to bend and catch hold of Joy Turner by the arms. Feeling herself being drawn upwards, she tried to retain her grip on Jill Hambling's throat and shake herself free from his grasp.

"Let go of her, Joy, she's beaten!" the blond commanded, shaking the red head until she released the older girl. Lifting her to her feet, although she looked to be on the verge of collapsing, he raised his voice and addressed the owner of the Longhorn Saloon. "Get those women in here to look after Jill, damn it, Barney!"

Von Lindeiner was making a terrible mistake by drawing attention to himself in such a fashion!

In spite of experiencing the kind of sexual stimulation which always came when watching a fight between women, the sight of the blond and, more particularly, the sound of his voice caused Ernst Kramer to realize something was *very* wrong!

With the stimulus of the action over, *der Fleischer's* earlier and ignored suspicion that he recognized the man who had started to rise when the fighting began in earnest was able to make itself felt.

A sense of grim foreboding came with the thought!

While the money paid for the "jewels" would have allowed the recipient to purchase his present attire, he could not have learned to speak English—particularly with such fluency—since that morning!

Yet, as his lack of knowledge had caused the need for an interpreter, there was no reason why the blond should have pretended to have only a most fragmentary knowledge of English at the hotel.

Unless——!

"Schmidt!" Kramer bellowed, so alarmed by the possibility which had just occurred to him that he could not prevent himself from speaking. He leapt to his feet, although he realized just too late that he was acting against his own best interests by doing so.

Hearing his assumed name and seeing who had spoken it, von Lindeiner released Joy. Giving her not so much as a glance as she crumpled limply on to her unconscious opponent, he spun on his heel and ran across the open space. While doing so, he pulled free the short barrelled revolver he was carrying in a shoulder holster. The weapon prevented anybody from trying to stop him as he hurdled the rope and made for the front entrance. Despite that, his attempt at flight was to no avail.

Showing commendable presence of mind, *der Fleischer's* bodyguard left by the side door as soon as he saw what was happening. He deduced correctly in which direction to go and intercept the fleeing blond. However, instead of trying to capture him so he could be questioned, the young man shot von Lindeiner in the head before he could reach the horses tethered outside the barn and steal one upon which to escape.

CHAPTER SEVEN

It's You Who're Doing the *Lying*

"Jewels!" Belle Starr repeated, in tones of convincing puzzlement, standing as tense as a bobcat confronted by a couple of hound dogs and studying the unwelcome visitors so she would be able to identify them later. "Which *jewels* are you talking about, for mercy's sake?"

"Don't try to play the god-damned innocent with *us*!" warned the shorter of the two men. Although lacking his companion's timbre of breeding and education, his voice established that he too was a Westerner. Possibly in his late forties, despite being equally well dressed, he looked less comfortable in such clothing. "Ike Fein told us you've got it and that's his gear on the sidepiece."

"Ike *wouldn't*—!" the brunette began to protest, but stopped as she realized that she was betraying herself.

"Ike not only *would*, young lady, he *did*," the taller of the pair claimed. While hard, his face was handsome and he was somewhat younger than the other man. His name, Belle discovered later, was Dexter Soskin and his companion was Tom Wylie. "But don't judge him too harshly. Anybody would have done it, with their feet sticking in a fire."

"The old son-of-a-bitch held out a heap longer than I reckoned he would," the shorter man supplemented, leering evilly at the lady outlaw as he was speaking. "Fact being, high-toned and fancy gal, I lost me ten simoleons betting Dex here how long it'd be afore he got around to talking."

"You lousy *bastards*!" Belle spat out furiously.

Despite appreciating that she was once more supplying confirmation of her association with Isaac Fein, the brunette was unable to prevent herself from doing so. In fact, being

64

able to visualize the kind of suffering which must have been inflicted upon the elderly and gentle receiver of stolen goods, she could barely control her urge to snatch out the modified Manhattan Navy revolver and try to avenge him. Nor did she blame him for having betrayed her. He must have been in terrible pain for him to have done so. In addition to being a trusted friend of long standing, he had supplied the means by which she could carry out the lucrative "diamond switch" confidence trick and she was also performing an assignment, the nature of which demonstrated how much faith he had in her, on his behalf.

Not all of the story which Belle had told Ernst Kramer was a lie. The genuine jewels she had displayed and tested were part of the loot stolen from the *Comtesse de* Saint-Pierre. As they had been mounted in such well known pieces, they were removed so that the easily indentifiable settings could be melted down and re-moulded before being offered for sale.

The lady outlaw had had no part in the theft. Nor, in spite of her explanation to *der Fleischer*, did she know by whom it had been committed. Her participation had come about as a result of a request for assistance from Fein, to whom she was obligated for help in the past. Having come into possession of the stones from a source he had not disclosed, nor into which had she felt the need to inquire, he had asked her to deliver them from his place of business in Chicago to a buyer who would come from Canada to a pre-arranged rendezvous. While the payment he had offered for the assignment was not particularly high, he had supplied the imitation jewels and the rest of the equipment required for her to be able to augment it by operating the confidence trick during the journey.

Knowing Fein as well as she did—he was, in fact, one of the few receivers of stolen goods for whom she had any respect—Belle felt sure he had believed he was speaking the truth when he had told her the delivery would be simple and could be accomplished without risk. If he had even suspected somebody was after the jewels, being a loyal friend in addition to having a considerable sum of money invested in the transaction, he would have warned her so that she could take the necessary precautions.

"*He* called us a whole heap worse than *that*," Wylie asserted, still wearing the sadistic grin, "afore he got 'round to telling us what we was after."

"I've no *idea* how this person you're talking about came to know me," Belle objected, restraining her impulse to find some way of wiping the leering expression from the speaker's face as painfully as possible. "But he was lying if he—!"

"It's you who're doing the *lying*, young lady," Soskin interrupted, with a smooth near-gentle tone which caused the brunette to consider him far more intelligent and, as a result of this, a greater potential danger than his uncouth companion. "You were seen putting the scales in your portmanteau and heard talking about pulling the 'diamond switch' on your way west. You were then followed to the railroad depot, watched buying a ticket to Ellsworth and boarding the train."

"She told us what you looked like, only not just how good you look," Wylie went on. "And's soon's Dex read what you'd put about 'valuating' jewels in the newspaper, he knew right off it was *you*'s we'd come after."

"*She*? Belle asked, playing for time as much as seeking information. "Which *she* would that be?"

Having been involved with criminals of various kinds all her life, the lady outlaw was not surprised by the discovery that her unwanted visitors had learned of Fein's transaction. She was all too aware of how even what should be carefully kept secrets had a way of becoming less confidential than was desirable. For all that, having seen and been impressed by the adequacy of Fein's security arrangements, which she had at his request tried without success to find a means of breaching, she wondered how the pair could have gained access to him and be able to inflict the torture. The shorter man's reference indicating a woman was implicated had supplied a clue not only to the most likely source of the leakage, but to how they had contrived to reach him. He had in his employ, ostensibly as his assistant in his pawnshop, a young and attractive girl. Belle could not envisage anybody else who could have been sufficiently in his confidence to be able to betray him. Certainly it could not have been his wife. In addition to being a bedridden invalid, she loved him dearly and knew nothing about his illicit activities.

"That gal's worked in his store and bedded down with him," Wylie replied, confirming the brunette's suspicions.

"I thought that's who it must be," Belle admitted, trying to keep the conversation going for long enough to let her decide upon a line of action which would allow her to turn the tables on the pair. "But why did she do it?"

"A mixture of jealousy, thwarted ambition and loss of money which she'd looked forward to getting her hands on," Soskin explained. "She was hoping to be allowed to deliver the jewels and didn't take kindly to finding out that Fein had asked a *shiksa*[1] like you to do it instead. It's a pity for Fein's sake that he didn't let her. She was going to hand them over to me and it would have saved him a lot of suffering. As it was, she had to let us in so we could learn everything we could about you the hard way."

"God damn the treacherous little bitch!" the lady outlaw said bitterly. "I'd like to get my hands on her!"

"You won't this side of hell," Wylie stated.

"So you've killed her?" Belle announced rather than asked, directing the words at the taller man.

"Of course," Soskin answered, speaking in a matter-of-fact fashion which did nothing to make the brunette revise her opinion of who was the more deadly of the pair. "I couldn't chance leaving her behind for Fein's friends to get their hands on and I had no intention of bringing her with me. So there was no other way out. She could put a name to me and you know what a vengeful bunch of bastards those Jews can be when one of their own's been killed."

"Is Ike dead too?" Belle breathed.

"He held out too long," Soskin replied, showing no more emotion than if making casual and unimportant conversation. "But I couldn't have left him alive, either."

"Oh my god!" Belle gasped, backing away from the men as if overcome by shock and horror at the news.

This was not entirely correct!

Despite having suspected from the beginning that the torturing of Fein might have ended in his death, the lady outlaw was distressed by finding out this had been the case. However, her emotions were far different from those she was displaying. Although she was seething with rage, she was sufficiently strong willed to hold it in check. Much as she wanted to

1. *"Shiksa": derogatory Jewish name for a young Gentile woman. J.T.E.*

avenge her friend, she also wished to continue living. She knew that only by remaining completely cool and collected could she hope to do so.

"Hell's fire, Dex, let's get on with it!" Wylie put in impatiently. "I've things I want to do tonight."

"Whatever you say, Tom," the taller man answered and stepped forward. "You might as well hand over the jewels, Miss Beauregard. We know you have them and it will save you some grief if you do."

Listening to the ultimatum, every instinct possessed by the brunette warned that surrendering the jewels would not save her from suffering a similar fate to the old man and the treacherous young woman. Aware of just how precarious her position was, she was thinking rapidly in an attempt to find some way by which she could survive.

Throughout the conversation, which the brunette counted herself extremely fortunate to have kept going for so long, she had been carefully studying the pair. Her summations about their respective natures were far from comforting. Unless her judgement was at fault and she had sufficient confidence in it to doubt this was the case, neither had the slightest respect for the sanctity of human life. The shorter man was a sadistic brute, deriving pleasure from causing suffering and killing. On the other hand, murder was no more than a means to an end where the other was concerned and, in her opinion, that was what made him by far the more dangerous of them.

There was, Belle considered, only one slender point in her favour!

Drawing conclusions from the employment by the taller man of a favourite alias she adopted when wishing to remain incognito,[2] the brunette felt sure neither Fein nor his betrayer —the latter because she had been unaware of it—had disclosed her true identity to the two men!

In which case, the pair could be less wary than if they knew they were dealing with Belle Star!

"All right, all *right*!" the lady outlaw gasped in a voice throbbing with well simulated submissive and terrified resignation, having halted almost against the wall and by the side

2. *Details of an occasion when Belle Starr employed the alias "Magnolia Beauregard" can be found in:* Case One, "The Set-Up," SAGEBRUSH SLEUTH. *J.T.E.*

of the bed. Thankful that Fein had given her alias and the two men were unaware of who they were up against, she went on in a similar fashion. "Don't hurt me, *please*! Here they are!"

While speaking, Belle had reached across to take the buckskin pouch in her right hand. She was holding it in such a fashion that she retained a grip on one end of the drawstring between her left thumb and forefinger. Giving an inconspicuous tug, she caused the oversized bow to demonstrate it had another purpose besides adding to the deception when the substitution was made in the confidence trick. It came apart easily, allowing the neck of the pouch to open. As soon as this happened, she tossed it so it fell before Soskin could reach out and catch it. On landing, its contents sprayed over the floor in a glistening flood.

Instantly, if involuntarily, the two men looked downwards!

What was infinitely more vital, as far as the lady outlaw's continued well being was concerned, the barrels of the Colts wavered out of alignment.

Throwing herself forward so she alighted facing the foot of the bed, Belle rolled across it with all the speed she could muster. While doing so, refusing to be distracted by the thought that it seemed much wider than when she had slept in it, she plunged her right hand into the reticule to close on the butt of the Manhattan Navy revolver.

Although the men brought up the Colts almost immediately and fired, the barrels were directed at the position already—if only just—vacated by the brunette and the bullets ploughed harmlessly into the wall.

Paying no attention to the shots, Belle continued to move with the kind of smooth co-ordination only long practise backed by nerves of steel could produce. By the time she was tumbling to the floor, she was holding the modified weapon with its hammer fully cocked. Furthermore, having no wish to be encumbered by it, she had liberated her left wrist from the carrying cord and left the reticule behind on the bed.

On landing, the brunette found that her, of necessity, rapid summation of the situation was correct. Not only could she see the taller and more dangerous man around the foot of the bed, but he was in his companion's line of fire.

There was not, however, even a split second to spare for self congratulation!

Grasping the Manhattan in both hands as an aid to aiming, Belle sighted and fired. Already Soskin was starting to swing his Colt towards her. Peering through the swirling white gasses of the detonated powder, she saw his head jerk and the derby hat torn from it. Releasing the revolver without firing, he spun around to sprawl face forward against the wall.

Even with his companion felled, the shorter man was still outside the brunette's range of vision. Nor, despite letting out a startled and profane threat, did he move into view. Neither did she attempt to rise from her place of concealment so as to be able to engage him in gun play. Instead, she remained where she had fallen and listened to what he was doing.

Shocked and not a little alarmed by having seen Soskin shot, Wylie's first thought was to get away from the room. Then his avaricious nature overcame his concern. While he realized that the sound of the shooting might bring people to investigate, he could not bear the thought of fleeing and leaving the glittering "jewels" behind. On the other hand, he was equally aware of the danger posed by the beautiful young woman who he had been considering as nothing more than a harmless victim. Unless the threat she offered could be nullified, he would not be able to gather up the loot.

With the latter thought uppermost in his mind rather than any idea of avenging his stricken companion, Wylie started to move forward. His attention was directed to the bed, watching for the first sign of the young woman appearing, until his forward foot descended on the second step. There was a crunching sound beneath it, far louder than he cared to contemplate as it might signal his intentions to the object of his activities and warn her of what he contemplated. Halting and raising his foot, he glanced down. The sight which met his gaze froze him into immobility.

"God damn it!" Wylie ejaculated, staring at the shattered remnants of a "diamond" and realizing what its destruction implied. "These aren't *real*!"

"I never said they *were*," Belle answered in a mocking tone which she hoped would goad the man into recklessness, having deduced what was happening from the sounds she had heard.

The hope did not come to fulfilment!

"Come out from behind there, you 'mother-something' whore!" Wylie commanded, having acquired too healthy a respect for the brunette's accuracy to behave in the way she wanted. Continuing to stand still, he decided such an attitude would achieve nothing and went on in a far from convincing tone of conciliation, "Tell you what, high-toned gal. Give me the real jewels and I'll light a shuck without hurting you."[3]

"I just *bet* you will, you murderous, yellow-bellied son-of-a-bitch!" Belle answered, still hoping to lead the killer into ill advised behaviour. "If you want them *that* badly, come and get them!"

While the conversation was taking place, the lady outlaw had taken her left hand from the revolver. Without moving any more than was absolutely necessary from her prone position, she raised the covers slightly and peered under the bed. She discovered, as she had feared, they extended so low all the way round that she was unable to see even the man's feet to supply a target at which to shoot.

However, something else caught Belle's eye and offered a possible solution to her dilemma!

Straining her ears so they would catch the first suggestion that the man was moving closer, the brunette reached out and gripped the handle of the empty chamber pot. Like all of the hotel's furnishings, it was of substantial construction. Lifting it from the floor, so she could move it silently, she swung and tossed it as hard as she could in her restricted position towards the other side of the bed. Awkward though her movements were compelled to be as a result of her precarious situation, she achieved her purpose.

What was more, the ploy worked!

Seeing the covers of the bed being agitated violently, Wylie drew the conclusion which Belle was hoping to create. Bringing his Colt around, he started shooting. Hurried as his action was, it proved effective. Not, however, in the way he desired. His two bullets flew true, striking and shattering the cause of

3. *For the benefit of new readers: "Light a shuck" is a cowhands' expression for leaving hurriedly. It derives from the habit in night camps of trail drives and round ups of supplying "shucks"—dried corn cobs—to be used for illumination by anybody who had to leave the camp fire and walk in the darkness. As the "shuck" burned away quickly, a person had to move fast if wanting to benefit from its light. J.T.E.*

the movement. Unfortunately for him, it was not as a result of the lady outlaw having tried to attain a firing position by crawling underneath the bed.

Thrusting herself into a kneeling posture the moment she heard the shots and the destruction of the chamber pot, Belle was once more grasping the butt of the Manhattan in both fists. Doing so allowed her to attain a greater accuracy than would have been possible with a single-handed hold and, when firing at speed, she could also more easily control the increased kick of the recoil caused by the modifications.

A snarled imprecation burst from Wylie as he realized his mistake, but he was given no chance to correct it.

Four times, as swiftly as Belle could operate the hammer and counter the effects of the powder charges in the successive chambers of the cylinder being ignited, her revolver barked sharply. She angled the shots slightly apart and all but the first ripped into the man's torso. Although the Colt boomed once, between the second and third discharges from the lighter weapon, its owner was already staggering under the impact of the round, .36 calibre, soft lead balls and its .44 bullet went into the door of the wardrobe. Then he was going down, dying and with the handgun flying from his inoperative fingers.

Rising from the kneeling posture, the brunette was on the point of cocking her Manhattan when she realized that doing so was pointless. Such had been the force of her previously held back anger over the torturing and murder of Fein, she had allowed herself to commit a possibly dangerous indiscretion.

Although resembling the Colt 1851 Navy Model revolver in construction and design,[4] with the exception of there being

4. *The Colt 1851 Navy Model revolver had a seven and a half inches' octagonal barrel, making it thirteen inches long and it weighed two pounds, ten ounces. As produced by its manufacturers, the Manhattan Navy's barrel was also octagonal, but an inch shorter, giving it an overall length of eleven and one half inches, with a weight of only two pounds. Although we did not learn of this until recently—how we came into possession of all the added information given in this volume is told in the Introduction to* THE JUSTICE OF COMPANY "Z"—*the Manhattan carried by Belle Starr in her reticule was made more suitable for concealment purposes by having its loading lever removed from beneath the barrel which was cut down to two inches. She also owned a second Manhattan of standard size and fittings which she carried when wearing a gunbelt and holster. For information regarding the reason .36 was termed the "Navy" and .44 the "Army" calibre, see:* Footnote 11, APPENDIX TWO. J.T.E.

a spring plate interposed between the nipples of the cylinder and the hammer—the purpose of which was to deflect the possible backflash when the cap was ignited—the Manhattan differed in one major aspect. Where the Colt was a "six-shooter," it was chambered for only five bullets.

Silently cursing her impulsive behaviour in emptying the Manhattan, the lady outlaw looked from one to the other of her would-be assailants. She was ready to dive for and try to collect one of the Colts if need be, but decided there was nothing further to fear from either man. Both were sprawled motionless on the floor.

Despite her conviction, Belle tossed the Manhattan on the bed and, picking up the revolver dropped by the taller man in passing, went to the door. Opening it and looking out, she neither saw nor heard anything to indicate that the shooting had attracted the attention of any other occupant of the building. Closing the door and thinking how fortunate it was that even the interior walls and floors of the hotel were constructed so sturdily, she hurried to the side window. Lifting the bottom half of the sash, she leaned out to gaze into the alley.

"What's up?" Sammy Crane called, having heard the gun play even though nobody inside the building had done so. He had drawn the correct conclusions from the lighter calibre weapon being the last to fire and had waited instead of dashing in to investigate.

"I'll tell you when I come down," Belle replied. "Catch my gear when I throw it out."

Dropping the Colt on to the bed near her own revolver as she passed, the brunette opened the door of the wardrobe. A lifetime's experience as an outlaw had taught her the advisability of always being ready to make a hurried departure when engaged in an illicit activity. With such a contingency in mind, she had only unpacked from her portmanteau the equipment required for the confidence trick and whatever garments she currently needed. Replacing the few items of clothing, she decided against carrying away the scales, metal plate, hammer and loupe. Nor did she intend to delay her departure by collecting the fake jewels scattered across the floor. The original owner of the tools had no further use for them and—as seemed likely—should Ernst Kramer learn of the deception, word of her activities would spread far too rapidly for her to be able to resume operations in the near future.

Closing and locking the portmanteau, Belle took it to the window. After checking with the waiting man that they were not being observed, she dropped it to Crane. Then collecting and returning the Manhattan to the holster built into the reticule, she left the room. Having locked the door, she walked down the stairs and dining-room to join him in the alley. Telling him what had taken place as they set off together, they made their way towards the rooming house to await Blue Duck's return with news of how his mission had turned out.

CHAPTER EIGHT

I Want the Bitch *Killed*

About thirty seconds after Belle Starr had locked the door, a low groan broke the silence which had descended upon the room and Dexter Soskin's body began to writhe spasmodically on the floor.

If the lady outlaw had been in less of a hurry to take her departure from the Columbus Grand Hotel, or had made a closer examination of her two unwanted visitors before leaving, she would have found she was in error with regards to their condition. While Tom Wylie was dead, his taller companion had had a very narrow escape from meeting a similar fate. The bullet she had fired at him merely grazed the side of his head in passing, stunning and knocking him down. As he was falling, he had turned and landed in such a position that she was prevented from seeing the actual extent of his wound. Having noticed his hat being knocked off, she had assumed his injury was more lethal than had been the case.

Soskin's return to full possession of his faculties took almost another minute. First struggling to his knees, he felt at the shallow groove carved across the side of his head and looked around. Finding that his intended victim was no longer present, which did not come as any great surprise, he turned his attention to his own welfare. Rising and supporting himself against the wall until his strength returned, he gazed about him to take stock of the situation. A single glance informed him, much to his relief, that his motionless companion would not be able to supply information to the town marshal when the results of their efforts were discovered.

Although he was unaware of exactly how long had elapsed since he was knocked unconscious, Soskin felt sure the beautiful young woman had not reported the incident to either the hotel's house detective or the local law enforcement officers. Instead, he deduced correctly that she had made good her escape. With that thought in mind, he concluded that he would be advised to do the same.

As Soskin was about to put his intentions into being, he noticed the glistening objects scattered on the floor. For a moment, he was puzzled by the sight. From what he recollected of the disparity between her earlier demeanour and subsequent most effective behaviour, he felt sure that the girl who Isaac Fein had called "Magnolia Beauregard" was possessed of far greater courage than he had been led to assume at first. It was most unlikely that she had fled in such a state of panic that she forgot, or dare not wait, to collect them. Which suggested they were not the genuine jewels, but merely some of the fakes used as substitutes in the "diamond switch" confidence trick. Seeing the shattered fragments which had alerted his now dead companion to the same possibility, his suspicions were confirmed.

"Which means you've still got the real stones," the wounded man growled, having had a sufficiently good education so that he did not need to lard his words with profanities to satisfy himself. He crossed to the sidepiece and looked in the mirror. "But I'm going to get them, if it's the *last* thing I do!"

Having delivered the sentiment, Soskin tried to clean his face with water from the jug on the washstand. He was unsuccessful. Although his wound was far from incapacitating, he could not stop the trickle of blood which oozed out of it and down his cheek. Realizing that to try and leave the hotel in such a condition would arouse unwanted interest and could lead to questions to which he would be unable to supply a satisfactory answer, he discarded the idea of making the attempt by the conventional means of exit.

Without bothering to try the door and so discover it was locked from the other side, Soskin went to collect Wylie's hat. His own was ruined and going out with no headdress could draw the kind of attention he wanted to avoid. Donning the derby and picking up his discarded Colt 1860 Army revolver from the bed as he went by, he crossed to the window. Looking out, he found no need for the weapon. Belle Starr and

Sammy Crane had already left the alley and nobody else was in sight to challenge his departure.

Lowering the rope supplied as a fire precaution, Soskin contrived to slide down it to the ground. Arriving safely, in spite of still being far from at the peak of health as a result of his very close escape from death, he set off in search of further information which he hoped would guide him to the exceptionally competent and beautiful young woman he knew as "Magnolia Beauregard."

Soskin would never know it, but his flight from the building was only just in time!

"Is Miss von Blücherdorf in yet?" demanded Ernst Kramer, striding to the reception desk of the Columbus Grand Hotel with his face suffused by a mixture of alarm and anger, followed by Jebediah Lincoln and his bodyguard.

Having supplied an acceptable reason for his behaviour and the killing of Franz von Lindeiner, which the owner of the Longhorn Saloon had not questioned because of suspecting that it was correct, *der Fleischer* had wasted no time in returning from the barn to Ellsworth. Nor had he stopped to inform the town marshal of his suspicion that he was the victim of a confidence trick. Instead, accompanied by Jebediah Lincoln and the second of his bodyguards, he had returned directly to his temporary accommodation with the intention of personally confronting the leading perpetrator of the fraud.

"I—I—I—!" the clerk began having watched the way in which Kramer entered the building and realizing that something of exceptional gravity was responsible for his all too obvious agitation.

"Well!" Kramer thundered, being experienced in the devious ways of employees in hotels when asked for information which they had been requested and possibly bribed not to divulge. "Is she, or *isn't* she?"

"Er—I—That is—!" the clerk commenced, glancing at the mail rack more to avoid meeting the irate guest's eye than for any other reason. However, as he did, he noticed something which he decided would enable him to temporize and, perhaps avoid antagonizing either his interrogator or "Miss von Blücherdorf." Looking across the desk once more, he continued,

"Well, sir, as her key isn't here, it's possible that she may be. Can I send up a bellboy—?"

"Bellhop be 'somethinged'!" *der Fleischer* refused furiously, employing the colloquial term for the type of employee in question as he did when he went on no less heatedly, "Get me the house peeper!"

"The—?" queried the clerk.

"God damn it!" Kramer snarled, being in such a state of agitation that he was only just able to avoid breaking into German. "Don't you have a house *detective* in this 'mother-something' hotel?"

"Oh yes, sir!" the clerk answered, glancing at the door of the office which had been assigned to the recently appointed retired peace officer who now served the hotel in such a capacity. As it was being opened he went on, somewhat huffily. "It's just that I've never heard the term you employed. Here comes our Mr. Crosby now."

"What's up, Mr. Blenny?" inquired the thickset, grizzled and hard faced hotel detective, having heard enough of the conversation through the door, which he always left slightly ajar, to know his services were required. He crossed the hall with the purposeful stride of one who meant to stand no nonsense, even from an obviously affluent and clearly irate guest.

"Come with me!" Kramer ordered, before the clerk could reply, starting to turn.

"What for—sir?" Crosby asked, his voice indicative of Western origins.

"I've been 'something-well' cheated is what for!" *der Fleischer* announced, halting his movement and directing a scowl at the house detective. "So——!"

"It'd be best was you to moderate your language and hold your voice down—*sir*," Crosby asserted, showing no sign of being perturbed by the guest's behaviour. "We don't want to attract too much attention, do we?" He paused, as if to let the other contemplate the wisdom of his words, before going on, "Who cheated you and how?"

"That 'mother-something' whore who calls herself 'Cornelia von Blücherdorf' was in on it," Kramer claimed, but in a much quieter voice as he appreciated the value of the advice about avoiding drawing unwanted interest his way even though he disregarded the request to refrain from employing profanities. "She and a Prussian son-of-a-bitch sold me some stolen jewels."

"Are you *sure* they were *stolen*?" Crosby wanted to know, as he set off towards the stairs with *der Fleischer* and the other two men.

"Of course I am, she as good as——!" Kramer commenced, but realized he was making an incriminating admission and revised it to something he felt would be more acceptable. "They wouldn't have let them go so cheaply if they'd been come by honestly."

"Are you sure they were *genuine* jewels?" the house detective challenged, his hard features giving no indication of how he regarded the revised explanation.

"She tested them——!" *der Fleischer* began, but stopped speaking as he appreciated how little credence could be placed upon the brunette's verification of the jewels if his suspicions were correct. "Hell, I'd seen the advertisement she put in the *Tribune* and thought she must be all right seeing's she was staying in this hotel."

"We don't check into our guests' backgrounds—*sir*—so long as they behave in a respectable fashion," Crosby pointed out, too wily in spite of his comparatively short period of employment in his present capacity to allow the suggestion of the hotel being culpable to go unchallenged. "Which the lady had done ever since she checked in. Do you reckon this Prussian feller will be with her?"

"No!" Kramer claimed definitely. "My man there killed him out at O'Bannion's barn. That's when I got to figuring out what had happened."

"Then she'll most likely be alone," Crosby estimated, as the group came to a stop outside the appropriate door. His voice took on a coldly commanding timbre as he continued, "I'll do *all* the talking and *anything* else that needs doing happen she's here."

"Kick it open, damn it!" *der Fleischer* ordered rather than requested, after several knocks by the house detective failed to elicit any response.

"There's no call for that," Crosby refused and took out his pass key. Unlocking and opening the door, he stepped inside. The sights which met his sweeping gaze brought him to a halt and he ejaculated, "Hot damn, here's *something* I hadn't counted on!"

"What's wrong?" Kramer asked, pushing forward.

"Looks like we're too late," Crosby answered, indicating the body, the glistening objects scattered on the floor, then the open side window with the fire escape rope passing through it. "Do you know him?"

"No," *der Fleischer* answered. "But he could be one of those pair I thought were beef heads when I saw them running away after they'd busted that window with a bullet."

"Oh sure, the day man told me about that when I came on," Crosby admitted, then he became businesslike and commanding. "Have one of your men go down and tell the desk clerk to send a bellhop for the marsh——What's up?"

"This looks like the bag the jewels I bought were in!" Kramer replied, striding forward with a profane exclamation to pick up the buckskin pouch.

"Where did you leave them?" Crosby inquired, hurrying to the side window and looking into the alley which Dexter Soskin had already vacated.

"In my room," *der Fleischer* replied. "The bank was closed when I got back from the railroad depot, but I left one of my men to guard them."

"You'd best have them fetched here to show the marshal," the house detective suggested, frowning, as he turned from the window. "Seems I recollect hearing tell of a trick that's pulled with real and fake jewels in bags that are look-alikes. Which those on the floor aren't likely to be real, else they wouldn't've been left behind."

"Unless *you* scared her off when you knocked at the door inst—!" Kramer objected.

"I didn't," Crosby declared, walking over to where the fake jewels were scattered. "There's nobody in sight out there. How about doing what I asked?"

"Go and tell the clerk to send for the marshal," Kramer barked at Lincoln. Then, taking a small bunch of keys and the one belonging to his suite from his jacket's pocket, but making no attempt to detach the other from his watchchain, he offered them to his bodyguard and commanded, "Fetch the cash box from my portmanteau."

While *der Fleischer* was delivering the instructions,

Crosby had gathered one of the "pearls" and a few fragments of the shattered "diamond." Before he could examine them, the hat discarded by Dexter Soskin attracted his attention. Going over and collecting it he studied for a moment the way in which the curly brim had been torn by the brunette's bullet. Then, dropping the objects he was holding into it, he crossed to and knelt alongside the body.

"God damn it!" Kramer complained, joining the house detective. "If we'd come straight up here—!"

"We'd still have been too late!" Crosby interrupted firmly, having touched the face of the corpse and having no intention of allowing the blame for the brunette's escape to be laid upon him. "This jasper's been dead for close to a quarter of an hour, which means whoever did it was gone before you came in and asked for me."

"Then why the 'something-hell' didn't *you* come to find out what was happening?" Kramer demanded.

"Because I didn't *know* anything had been," Crosby answered, straightening up and pointing at the body. "Sure he's been shot three times, but it was with something lighter than that Army Colt there and you could shoot off something even heavier than *that* without being heard outside the room, way this hotel's built. You said there were two fellers outside when the window was bust?"

"Mr. Kramer!" bellowed the bodyguard, throwing open the door and bursting in before the question could be answered. "I've just found Franz unconscious on the floor—."

Letting out a bawl of such alarm that it was practically incoherent, *der Fleischer* did not wait to hear any more. Rushing out of the room and along the passage, he was followed by his informant and Crosby. Goaded to a greater than usual alacrity by his sense of foreboding, he was still well ahead of them when he entered his suite. Paying not the slightest attention to the motionless form on the floor, his speed did not diminish until he entered the main bedroom. Skidding to a halt, one glance at the open cash box confirmed his fears. Then he noticed the writing on the sheet of paper and crossed to the sidepiece to pick it up.

"Dear Mr. Kramer," the red faced man read, the shaking of his hands growing greater as his fury increased with each word. "As the jewels I let you buy really were part of the

Comtesse de Saint-Pierre's collection, my conscience won't allow me to leave you in possession of stolen property. However, under the circumstances and as I cannot return you the money you paid, nor feel obligated so far as my commission is concerned, I feel it advisable to decline your kind offer to take dinner. Nor do I wish to continue our association. Yours sincerely, Cornelia von Blücherdorf. P.s. Please don't be too harsh with your young man. I'm afraid I lied to him. As I don't care to drink alone, I said you had told me in your note to come up and ask him to keep me entertained until you returned. C.v.B."

Snarling profanities in two languages, *der Fleischer* crumpled the paper into a ball and flung it to the floor. Stalking into the sitting-room, he was prevented from attacking the unconscious bodyguard by the arrival of the marshal. Although he made no attempt to inflict the summary punishment after the peace officer departed half an hour later, his temper was not improved.

Examining the bedroom of the suite and the brunette's quarters, the marshal had been far from optimistic. Overlooking the possibility of Kramer having purchased the jewels knowing them to be stolen, he had said that the dead man was not known to himself or Crosby and he promised to try and locate the other two people who were involved. Having drawn similar conclusions from the condition of the discarded derby, he had agreed with the house detective's suggestion that the shooting had happened as a result of a quarrel; perhaps over the division of the loot. Warning Kramer to stay in town until the sheriff of Ellsworth County had asked questions about the shooting of "Franz Schmidt," he had left to commence the search for "Cornelia von Blücherdorf" and the man he, like Crosby, assumed had been in the room with her.

"Much good *that* will do!" *der Fleischer* snarled, as soon as he and Lincoln had the dining-room of the suite to themselves. "Seeing how she took *me*, that 'mother-something' whore is way too smart for a country hick like him!"

"Do you want me to get the Pink-Eyes after her, boss?" the freighter suggested.

"What the hell for?" Kramer snarled.

"They could find her and fetch her back," Lincoln pointed out.

"Fetch her back be 'somethinged'!" *der Fleischer* spat back viciously. "I want the bitch *killed!*"

"*Killed*," Lincoln repeated. "But *that* won't get the jewels and money back for you."

"Those god-damned jewels are stolen property which the Pink-Eyes are already looking for!" Kramer exclaimed impatiently. "And, if she gets away from this 'mother-something' town, she'll probably have spent most of the money before they could get her. Besides, no 'something-or-other' whore's going to make a sucker out of *me* and live to enjoy it!"

"Hey!" the freighter ejaculated, slapping a fat hand against his right thigh. "I'm pretty near certain I saw Jubal Framant getting off the east-bound train. Put the right sized bounty on her head and he'll get her if *anybody* can."

"Go find him and fetch him here!" *der Fleischer* ordered. "I'll make him an offer he'll be only too willing to take."

"You're sure you know what I want you to do?" Belle Starr inquired.

It was shortly after noon on the day following the pulling of the "diamond switch" confidence trick and the sequence of violence and bloodshed which it had triggered off. Although Ernst Kramer would have taken no pleasure if he had known it, the lady outlaw had justified his belief that the town marshal would not catch her.

Having been told what had happened to Franz von Lindeiner by Blue Duck, who had arrived at the barn just too late to save him from being shot and who had remained to ensure he was dead before returning with the news, Belle had decided a change of location was needed. The owner of the Longhorn Saloon had introduced her part-Cherokee companions to the Prussian, in response to her request for an assistant who could help with the confidence trick. Should he be questioned by the sheriff about his association with von Lindeiner, he might say something to suggest where she might be found. The owner of the rooming house was an old friend whom the brunette had no desire to incriminate.

While Blue Duck and Sammy Crane had kept watch, Belle had changed her appearance to become the red haired saloongirl who had sought for information concerning Jubal Framant. Then, having packed all their belongings, she and the two men went to a small hotel on the opposite side of the railroad tracks to the more luxurious establishment she had patronized since arriving in Ellsworth. After they had settled in their new accommodation, they had gone around the town to see what could be learned about the situation.

What Belle and the men had discovered was not conducive to peace of mind, or complacency. While the evidence suggested nobody was aware of her true identity, she had found out that her victim was not a cattle buyer as she believed. He was a wholesaler of meat, but his major source of income was derived from the clandestine sale of firearms in large quantities, to purchasers with whom reputable companies would not deal.[1] A far greater cause for concern had been the discovery that he had had a meeting with Jubal Framant. It had not taken a great deal of thought to guess why.

Despite knowing Isaac Fein was dead, Belle intended to carry out the delivery. There was more than her personal integrity behind the decision, although this would have been sufficient inducement. By doing so, she would ensure that his widow received a good sum of money. However, being aware of how competent Framant had proved in the past, she had wanted to try and cover her tracks as much as possible. The means she had elected to employ would serve two ends. In the first place, there would be a false trail for him to follow. Secondly, it would reduce the chance of him learning too much should von Lindeiner have been indiscreet.

Brought to meet Belle by Blue Duck, Joy Turner had been willing to accept the proposition which was put to her. The result of the genuine fight, which Jill Hambling was supposed to have won, had made her unpopular with the owner of the saloon. As she was short of money, Barney Maters having refused to give her the sum promised on the grounds that he had had to pay off the wagers he had taken in the expectancy of her losing, she was not averse to receiving the necessary financial aid to leave. Nor had she been deterred by the lady

---

1. *As is recorded in,* THE REMITTANCE KID, *although Ernst 'der Fleischer' Kramer does participate personally in the events recorded in,* THE DEVIL GUN, *it was he who supplied the Agar Coffeemill Gun—an early and moderately successful type of weapon capable of automatic fire—which gives the title to that volume.* J.T.E.

outlaw warning her of the potential dangers, but agreed that the precautions which were to be taken should reduce these as far as possible.

"Yes," the red head replied. "I go with Blue Duck and Sammy Crane, pretending to be you, Miss von Blücherdorf."

"That's it," Belle agreed, having decided it was advisable to keep her real identity secret. "Keep it up for a full month if you can, but should anything go wrong, tell them the truth. That I paid you to do it and you don't know where I've gone."

Even if the last assumption should prove incorrect, the lady outlaw was confident the two men would prevent Joy from divulging the information to anybody until she was at least well on her way to the rendezvous. She was gambling upon the delay being long enough for the delivery to be made and she was free to make good her escape.

Belle also hoped that the waiting period in Elkhorn, Montana Territory, would not be extended, and would be uneventful.

CHAPTER NINE

You-All Having Trouble

A veritable cloud of profanity crackled around Miss Martha Jane Canary as she stood, hands on hips, glaring at the left front wheel of her wagon. It had sunk through the caved-in roof of a prairie-dog's hole. Having studied the situation, she slowly raised her eyes to study the setting sun. Estimating how much daylight remained, she let out a low groan. With all the West to pick from as a burrowing ground, it struck her as the height of misfortune that the animal should have elected to sink his home directly on the route she was taking. Of course, it might be claimed that the prairie-dog had been there first and she ought to have avoided its hole, but she felt disinclined to concede the point in her present and far from amiable frame of mind.

"God-blast your ornery, worthless, hole-grubbing hide!" Miss Canary spluttered, all her full vocabulary of profanities having lost their savour. "The hosses'll never haul it out, and night's near on here. I may's well make camp and cook up a meal. So keep out of sight, prairie-dog, or you'll be the meal's sure's my name's 'Calamity Jane'!"

Although few people would have known the speaker by her full name, the sobriquet she had used was already becoming famous despite her having only just attained eighteen years of age. Soldiers in the Army's string of forts claimed her acquaintance. Numerous drivers of freight wagons asserted, with few exceptions erroneously, to have taught her how to handle a bull whip. More than one saloon-girl now knew it paid to sing low when Calamity Jane entered her place of employment.[1]

1. *Details of the career and special qualifications of Miss Martha "Calamity Jane" Canary are given in:* APPENDIX ONE. *J.T.E.*

Five foot seven in height, the girl had a U.S. Cavalry kepi perched at a jaunty angle on her head. Her shortish, curly mop of red hair framed a face which was tanned, freckled, pretty and generally merry. Having matured early, her breasts rose round and full to force against the material of a well worn, fringed buckskin shirt which was open far enough from the neck to present a tantalizing glimpse of the top of the valley between the mounds. Trimming at the waist without artificial aids, her torso expanded to form curvaceous hips which fitted snugly into buckskin pants and were set on sturdily eye-catching legs. She had Pawnee moccasins on her feet and the rolled-up sleeves of her shirt exposed tanned arms more muscular than a lady of fashion would have cared for. Not that she had ever pretended to be one. An ivory handled Colt 1851 Navy revolver rode butt forward in the low cavalry twist holster on the right side of her well-made gunbelt. The handle of a coiled, long-lashed bull whip was thrust through the leather loop on the left side of the belt around her waist. Neither this, the handgun, nor the Winchester Model of 1866 carbine in the boot on the wagon's box were mere affectations. She could use all of them with considerable competence and ability.

"I'll just get the fire going afore I unhitch you, boys," Calamity told her two-horse team. "Maybe somebody coming along the trail over there'll see the flames and drop by to lend us a hand."

Collecting wood and dried buffalo "chips" from the rawhide "possum belly" under the wagon, the girl built a fire with the deft ease of one long accustomed to performing such a task. Filling her battered coffeepot with water from the butt on the side of the vehicle, she was setting it to boil on the flames when she saw that the possibility she had mentioned to the animals had taken place. Coming over a rim, a rider turned from the trail towards which she had been making when the accident occurred. As he was approaching, she hooked her thumbs into the gunbelt and subjected him to a careful, rangewise scrutiny.

Sitting his magnificent seventeen hand bloodbay stallion lightly, no mean feat for one who would top six foot three even when barefoot, the newcomer had the tremendously wide shouldered, slim waisted, well proportioned, muscular development of a Hercules. Having shoved back his costly white

low crowned, wide brimmed J.B. Stetson hat to display
golden blond hair, she could see he was blue eyed and had a
strong, tanned, almost classically handsome face. Rolled
tightly and knotted, a scarlet silk bandanna trailed long ends
down the front of an expensive fawn shirt. Although the cuffs
of the legs were turned back and hung outside his high heeled,
sharp toed boots, his trousers were made of a higher priced
material than the usual Levi's pants. They and the shirt had
clearly been made to his measure. His massive frame could
never have been fitted so well from the shelves of any store,
no matter how well stocked. About his middle hung a brown
gunbelt carved in a floral patterning and with two ivory handled Colt 1860 Army revolvers in its holsters. It was a rig
created by a master craftsman, one who knew exactly what
was needed to ensure an exceptionally rapid withdrawal of the
weapons in the hands of an expert.

Despite being something of a dandy dresser, the blond's
clothing was strictly functional and he exuded an air of quiet
self reliance. He was clearly at home on the range, although
his home range was almost certainly far to the south of Montana Territory.

"Texan," Calamity mused, having studied the shape of the
hat and noticed that the bloodbay's saddle was equipped with
the double cinches which were always used by citizens of the
Lone Star State. "Cowhand and a real good 'n', less I miss my
guess. Fact being, was them Army Colts carried for a cross
draw, I'd chance putting a name to you."

Regardless of her thoughts on the newcomer's possible
identity, the girl did not relax her vigilance as he brought his
horse to a halt a few yards from her. Allowing its reins to
dangle free and "ground hitch" it as effectively as if they were
tied to a rail, he strolled forward. Doffing his hat in an effort-
lessly gallant fashion, he nodded towards the wagon.

"Howdy, ma'am. You-all having trouble?"

"*Naw*!" Calamity snorted, too annoyed by what was an
embarrassing predicament for an experienced driver to con-
gratulate herself upon drawing the right conclusions as to his
origins. The blond giant's drawling accent had confirmed her
suppositions. "I just natural' like sitting here with a wheel all
bogged down and my son-of-a-bitching wagon stuck. 'Course
I'm not in any god-damned *trouble*!"

"That being the case," the Texas drawled calmly, his deep voice implying he had had a good education. "I'll be on my way. *Adios*."

Calamity stared at the big blond for a moment. Then a profanity ripped from her as, replacing the hat, he turned his back on her. Twisting palm out, her right hand enfolded the butt of the Navy Colt. Bringing it from its holster, she drew back the hammer with her thumb in the hope of making him halt.

"Hold it!" the red head yelled, when the clicking of the mechanism being brought to fully cocked produced no discernible result. Despite realizing that she could be acting in an unwise manner, she continued heatedly, "You come back here and bear a hand with the wagon, or I'll put lead into your Johnny Reb hide."

"Say 'please,'" the Texan requested, pausing and glancing over his shoulder.

"Do you *know* who I am?" Calamity demanded, her quick temper refusing to be cooled by the saner portion of her brain warning her that she should do so.

"No, ma'am."

"The name's Canary! *Martha Jane* Canary! Which, happen you're so all-fired, god-damned uneddicated, spells *Calamity Jane*——And means I'm Wild Bill Hickok's gal!"

If the girl expected her introduction—or fear of incurring the wrath of the famous James Butler "Wild Bill" Hickok—would bring the Texan to a condition of servile obedience, she was to be disappointed.

"Which same's as good a reason's I know for not helping you," the blond giant answered, tapping the Stetson to the correct "jack-deuce" angle over his off eye with the forefinger of his right hand and starting to walk once more. "I've never took to Wild Bill any ways at all."

"Hold it, damn you!" Calamity howled, and fired a shot, the bullet hissing just over the Texan's head.

This time the girl produced a reaction, but it was not the one she wanted!

While Calamity was still controlling the recoil of her weapon, the blond giant swung around with remarkable agility for one so large. What was more, he completed the turn holding a cocked Army Colt—in his *left* hand.

Calamity had been watching the Texan's right hand, knowing that most men who carried two guns did so in order to have twelve shots available instead of just six. The Army Colt might be as fine a percussion-fired revolver as any ever made, but it still took time to reload with combustible cartridges and even longer when using a powder flask and separate balls. Only a few men could handle the left side weapon with any facility. It was, she told herself, in keeping with her current lousy luck that she should meet one who was able to do so with great skill.

Even as the girl was drawing the conclusion, flame spurted from the blond giant's Colt. Fast as the shot was taken, dirt erupted between her feet and caused her to take a hurried, if involuntary, bound to the rear.

"Leather it!" the Texan commanded, cocking the Colt on the recoil. "Or I'll trim your toenails off to knee-level!"

"Wild Bill's not going to take kind to *this*!" Calamity warned, having no doubt that the threat could come close to being carried out and that the bullet which caused her retreat had struck within a couple of inches of where it had been directed.

While speaking, the girl twirled her revolver on the triggerguard and, twisting it around, flipped it back into the holster. Although she did not say the words, her attitude implied, "And that'll show you *how* to handle a gun!"

"Which same, looking at your wagon," the Texan answered calmly, "It'll be a fair spell afore you-all can go snitch to him about me."

At the conclusion of the comment, the big blond's Colt spun on his triggerfinger in a rapid motion. Then, seemingly of its own volition, it pinwheeled into the air so its barrel slapped into his palm. From there, the weapon curled around his hand, rose into the air again, turned to be caught by the butt and went back into the holster.

Despite her temper, Calamity was very impressed by what she had just seen. Being acquainted with a few prominent members of the gun-fighting fraternity, if on less intimate terms than she frequently claimed, she was not unfamiliar with the new and honorable art of pistol juggling. It was not, she realized, merely a show-off stunt; but served as a means of improving dexterity and strengthening the hands and wrists.

Her annoyance at the Texan notwithstanding, she was willing to concede his brief display equalled the best she had seen.

"Hey!" the girl yelled, watching the blond start to turn. "What in hell do I have to do afore you'll help?"

"Like I said, say 'please.'"

"You wouldn't want me to make it '*Pretty* please,' would you?"

"*Adios*," the Texas drawled, stepping forward.

"All right, blast you!" Calamity almost wailed, so intrigued by the blond giant that she was willing to curb her temper in the hope of prolonging their acquaintance. "Please, damn you. *Please!*"

"Now that's a whole heap *better*," the Texan declared with a grin, swinging to face the girl. "World'd be a happier place happen we all asked each other politely."

"And I hope Wild Bill asks you polite when he blows your blasted ears off for what you done to me!" the red head stated.

"Which's be the only way he could do it, gal," the Texan asserted, then glanced around. "There's nothing hereabouts we can use as a lever—"

"Which same I saw hours back, you danged knobhead!" gasped the even more aroused Calamity. "So what're *you* fixing to do about it?"

"Think some, first," the blond replied, seeming to grow calmer as the girl's ire increased. "What'd Wild Bill do?"

"He'd lay hold of that wheel and heft the whole blasted wagon up!"

"Would, huh? Have you-all any more logs in the possum belly?"

"These do?" Calamity inquired, reaching into the receptacle for fuel and producing three thick pieces of timber.

"Why sure," the Texan assented. "Get set to slide them in under the wheel."

"How?" the girl challenged. "Or are you kin to that goddamned prairie-dog and aim to dig the wheel out with your paws. Some stinking light-fingered varmint stole my shovel last time I was in Hays."

"Wasn't *Wild Bill* there to keep watch on it for you?" the blond giant inquired.

Only by making an effort of will was Calamity able to refrain from hurling the logs at the speaker. She had considerable knowledge of men, far more than a girl her age in more conventional circles would have acquired in a lifetime, but she had never come across one quite like him. He certainly knew the best way to rub her up the wrong way and get her pot-boiling mad.

After waiting for a few seconds for some comment, when none was forthcoming the blond giant walked to the wagon. Having studied it for a moment from the side, he looked beneath the canopy. Returning, he placed his back to the sunken wheel and, bending his legs slightly, hooked his hands under two of the spokes.

"Quit *trying*, feller!" Calamity advised. "Not even *Wild Bill* could lift that wagon of mine."

The handsome Texan did not deign to reply. Standing against the wheel, he took a firmer grip and slowly put on pressure. For close to thirty seconds, nothing happened apart from his face showing strain and setting into lines of grim determination. Sweat began to flow and the material of the shirt moved until it was made taut by the pressure causing the mighty muscles it covered to expand and harden.

Watching what was happening, Calamity opened her mouth to warn of the foolishness of any lesser mortal attempting something beyond the capability of even mighty Wild Bill Hickok.

The words went unsaid!

Before the girl's astonished gaze, the wagon began to move. Shifting slowly, but inexorably, its wheel rose from the hole. Putting all thoughts of Wild Bill from her mind, she moved into a position from which she could insert the logs.

"Just a mite higher, friend!" Calamity requested, kneeling by her rescuer's side and lowering one of the logs towards the hole. The wheel continued to move upwards until she was satisfied and said, "Easy now! Can you hold it there?"

With his breath hissing through slightly parted lips and every muscle of his giant frame concentrating upon the effort, the Texan made no attempt to reply. Instead he braced himself more firmly and did as was requested. He gave the impression that he might be posing for a painting of some legendary clas-

sic hero performing a superhuman feat of strength. Lacking
the standard of education necessary to draw such a conclusion,
as the girl glanced upwards, she decided he looked like one
hell of a man.

Not that Calamity wasted much time in staring. Being extremely practical, if inclined to be a mite hot-headed, she
knew there would be limits to her helper's Herculean strength.
Therefore, she must have the logs in position before the
weight he was supporting became too much for him and he
was compelled to lower it.

"Lower away, friend!" the girl ordered, having situated the
supports to her satisfaction in the hole.

By bending his legs slowly, the Texan allowed the weight
to settle gradually instead of letting it drop as most men would
have done. Not that many men could have lifted the wagon in
the first place. Watching the vehicle descending, Calamity
was holding her breath and biting her lip in anxiety. If the logs
did not hold, she would be to blame and not the blond giant.
She had no desire to hear what he would say if she failed in
her part of the removal after he had succeeded so admirably in
his own.

The support for the wheel held!

Springing to the heads of the horses with a gasp of relief,
Calamity looked at the big Texan. He stepped away from the
wagon. Turning to face it, he stood with his head hanging and
his chest heaving as he drew great gulps of air into his lungs.

"Giddap!" the girl yelled, pulling on the horses' headstalls.
"Come on, you no-good, slab sided, wored-out and worthless
apologies for crowbait. Pull!"

Throwing their weight against the harness, the animals
began to obey. The wagon rolled forward, stuck for a moment
as the wheel hit the rim of the hole. There was a lurch and the
onwards movement was resumed.

"Hold it! Throw back on those god-damned horses, you
fool female!"

Such was the fury of the bellow which left the Texan's lips
that, without meaning to, Calamity obeyed. Hot and angry
words bubbled inside her. She did not take kindly to being
addressed in such a fashion by any man, even if she was
beholden to him for helping her out of a tricky situation.

"What's eating *you*?" the girl demanded grudgingly, barely able to restrain the impulse to set the horses moving again.

"Let us not drop the *back* wheel into the hole this time," the blond giant suggested in a sardonic tone which did nothing to improve Calamity's feelings. "Who-all taught you to drive, *Wild Bill*?"

"You wait, mister, just you god-damn *wait*!" the red head thought.

For all her indignation, Calamity was almost writhing with shame. She had forgotten something which should have been obvious to even the rawest cook's louse in a freight outfit. Being herself, she decided the Texan was to blame for her lapse of memory over the vitally important matter of ensuring that the rear wheel did not plunge into the hole with a violence which might displace the logs and bog down the wagon once more.

Stamping each foot down angrily, the red head returned and studied the situation. She realized that the warning had not come a moment too soon. Another second and the wheel would have been into the hole. Muttering under her breath, she drew another log from the possum belly and added it to the support. Then, to make even more sure, she packed some soil around the logs.

"Well!" Calamity challenged, straightening up and eyeing the watching man defiantly. "Does *that* suit you?"

"Reckon it'll have to," the Texan replied. "Give her a whirl and we'll see."

The blond giant's demeanour came close to pushing the red head's temper beyond its limits. Turning on her heel, she almost threw herself towards the horses and gripped the reins of the nearer. Common sense returned as soon as she felt the leather in her grasp. Instead of starting the animals with a jerk which might have undone all they had achieved, she caused the vehicle to be eased forward inch by inch. As the wheel reached the logs, she leaned sideways to watch what was happening.

"Keep it going easy, gal!" the Texan encouraged, all the banter having left his voice, also studying the movement of the wagon.

Reaching the edge of the hole, the wheel dipped and stuck

for a moment. Then, yielding to the steady onwards pull of the team, it passed over and lifted on to solid ground. The wagon was clear of the obstruction and free to continue its journey.

CHAPTER TEN

Who *Is* Wild Bill Hickok?

"By cracky, mister, I wouldn't've believed it if I hadn't seen you do it," Calamity Jane declared, halting the vehicle and thinking how fortunate she was not to have been driving her more massive Conestoga wagon as raising it in such a fashion would be beyond even the tremendous strength of her gigantic rescuer.[1] Thanks."

"Think nothing of it," the Texan replied, then nodded towards the fire. "Would that be a coffeepot I see boiling up?"

"It surely would," the girl confirmed. "Set and rest up a spell while I unhitch my team, then I'll cook us both up a mess of victuals."

"That's right neighborly of you-all," the blond giant asserted. "Fact being, I was figuring on finding some place to bed down for the night when I saw you."

"Here'd be as good a place's anywhere around," Calamity remarked, in an off-hand tone which held neither a promise nor concern over having a stranger so close to her intended camp. "Fire's going already and, even if I say it's *should*, I'm a pretty fair hand at cooking."

"*Gracias*, I'll take you up on your kind offer," the Texan replied. "But I've never been one for standing 'round and watching a lady working. So I'll 'tend to my horse while you're unhitching and cooking."

After attending to his bloodbay stallion, the blond giant carried his saddle and the bedroll he had unstrapped from its

1. *The time would come when Mark Counter had cause to lift a much larger and heavier wagon, but he was helped by a man who could almost equal him in size and strength. The circumstances are described in:* THE GENTLE GIANT. *J.T.E.*

cantle to the side of the fire. Dropping the latter, as no cow-hand worth his salt would *ever* chance damaging his rig by standing it on its skirts, he set the former down on its right side. Doing so caused the Wincheser Model of 1866 rifle in the saddleboot to be on top and available should it be needed.

With the needs of the horse satisfied, the Texan walked across and offered to help Calamity complete the unhitching of the team. Her first instinct was to refuse, but she decided he was likely to take her at her word and she was eager to get the task finished so she could prepare and eat a meal.

"Going to say something?" the big blond inquired.

"Sure," the girl replied, annoyed that her rescuer had noticed she was about to speak and went on with the first thing to come into her mind. "I told you my name—!"

"And now you're wanting to know mine?" the Texan guessed.

"*Me*, heh!" Calamity snorted, tossing her head back in an entirely feminine manner which failed to produce any response from the person at whom it was directed. "All right, keep it to yourself happen you're so minded."

"The name's 'Counter,'" the blond giant introduced. "My *amigos* call me 'Mark.'"

It said much for the red head's ability as a poker player that she was able to prevent her mixture of surprise and annoyance from showing. When she had first seen him and deduced he was a Texas cowhand of the first water, she had thought her rescuer might be Captain Dustine Edward Marsden "Dusty" Fog. Discovering he did not wear his Army Colts in cross draw holsters had shown her she was in error. However, with that much of a clue, she ought to have realized his true identity. Mark Counter's name had long been connected with that of Dusty Fog.[2] One other point struck her. If, as rumor claimed, the Rio Hondo gun wizard was larger and stronger than his *amigo*, he must be a veritable giant.

"Right pleased to know you," Calamity said, trying to sound nonchalant as she had no wish for the big Texan to guess she was impressed by meeting with him.

2. *Details of Mark Counter's career and special qualifications, also pertaining to his association with Captain Dustine Edward Marsden "Dusty" Fog are given in:* APPENDIX TWO. *J.T.E.*

What was more, the girl realized Mark had not been merely boasting when he claimed he was indifferent to the possibility of incurring Wild Bill Hickok's wrath. She remembered the latter had left the town of Hays, where he was employed as marshal, to go hunting the day before the OD Connected ranch's trail drive had arrived the previous year. Or that was the reason he had given and, being a friend—albeit not on as close terms as she often implied—she had seen no cause to doubt his explanation.[3]

With the two horses unhitched and hobbled so they could graze with the bloodbay, Calamity set about preparing a meal. No matter how hot-headed she could be, she was an excellent cook. Neither she nor her guest spoke much while they were eating. Having finished and washed up the dishes, she walked over to where the Texan was standing.

"You're sure a mean hand with a skillet, Calam-gal," Mark said, grinning down at her. "Don't tell me Wild Bill taught you?"

Although the girl had been willing to bury the hatchet, the comment caused her to revise the decision. Despite being grateful for the big blond's assistance, she felt it incumbent upon her to teach him who was boss around *her* camp fire.

"I'm *Wild Bill's* gal!" Calamity asserted and swung the flat of her right hand against the blond's cheek with all her strength.

It was a good slap, the red head admitted to herself, but maybe a mite harder than she had intended and——

Shooting out, Mark's big hands clamped on the girl's shoulders and jerked her forward to be enfolded in his arms. Then he bent his head and his lips crushed against hers. Letting out a muffled gasp, she tried to twist her head away. Her hard little fists beat a tattoo against his shoulders, but he ignored them. Twisting his body without releasing the hold or halting the kiss, he took her left knee on his thigh as it drove up instead of allowing it to reach its intended target. Then he released and pushed her away.

3. *Miss Martha "Calamity Jane" Canary's last meeting with James Butler "Wild Bill" Hickok is described in:* Part Seven, "Deadwood, August 2nd, 1876," J.T.'S HUNDREDTH *and some of the events which led to the meeting are recorded in,* Part Six, "Mrs. Wild Bill," J.T.'S LADIES. *J.T.E.*

Standing for a moment, gasping for breath and red faced, Calamity stepped forward to deliver another slap and a repetition of the fiction with regards to her relationship to Wild Bill Hickok. Again the blond giant hauled her to him and crushed a kiss on her lips. When she was released, she staggered a pace or so to the rear and once more replenished her lungs.

"God damn you!" the girl gasped, her breasts heaving and, as she launched a third attack which was lacking the power of its predecessors, went on almost breathlessly, "I'm *Wild Bill's* gal!"

On the fourth, fifth and sixth slaps and kisses, Calamity's struggles grew progressively more feeble. What was more, she found herself kissing back.

"I—I'm—st—still—W—Wild B—Bill's—g—gal!" the red head almost moaned, after the seventh embrace, reeling on wobbly legs to direct a blow which barely touched the Texan's cheek.

For the eighth time, Mark scooped Calamity into his arms. On this occasion, her lips sought his, hungrily responding to the kiss with her tongue creeping into his mouth. Instead of flailing, her arms crept around him and her fingers dug into the hard muscles of his back. Nor did she resist as he lifted and carried her to where she had spread her bedroll beneath the wagon.

The night was dark, with only stars shining in the heavens. Only the usual sounds of the range broke the silence; the stamping of the blond giant's stallion as it heard the distant scream of a cougar; a thrashing as one of the girl's team rolled on the grass; the screech of a burrowing owl as it skimmed through the sky in search of prey.

Beneath the wagon, a large black mound separated to become two smaller mounds from the larger of which a masculine voice spoke.

"What do you-all think of Wild Bill Hickok *now*?"

A feminine voice, gentle, almost dreamily satisfied and contented replied from the smaller.

"Wild Bill Hickok—Who *is* Wild Bill Hickok?"

Creeping upwards in the east, the sun peeped over the horizon from which Mark Counter had ridden to Calamity Jane's assistance. Soon the cold grey light of dawn began to replace the blackness of the night sky.

Under the wagon, the blond giant stirred and, opening his eyes, he lifted his head from the pillow he always carried in his bedroll. Beside him, the girl moved sleepily, her bare arm around his equally unclad shoulders. Putting up his hand, he gingerly felt at the oval lump which had not been on the right side of his neck when he bedded down the previous night. A grin twisted at his lips as he concluded that his bandana would conceal it and, if not, he reckoned he was big enough to cope with any adverse comments about what he considered was a honourably acquired injury.

Two arms wrapped around Mark's neck as he was drawing the conclusion and a hot little mouth crushed against his, worked across his cheek and reached his ear.

"Mark!" Calamity breathed.

"It's time we were up and on our way, gal."

"Please—*pretty* please!"

Like the man said, the blond giant mused, a feller's sins always bounced right bac . on his fool head happen he stayed around long enough after committing them. After all, he had taken the firm stand on politeness bringing its own reward when he first met the red head. Being a Texas gentleman, there was only one thing he could do.

Half an hour later, Mark sat drawing on his boots. At his side, a look of contentment on her face, Calamity buttoned her shirt after having tucked it into her pants.

"Yes, sir!" the girl declared, rising and going to start making a fire. "World's sure a happier place happen we all ask each other real polite."

Thinking back to the night she had lost her virginity, Calamity remembered how she had imagined the man with whom it had happened would marry her. Only he had not. In fact, they had gone their separate ways the next morning. Or rather, he had taken his departure before she awoke. She had thought her heart would break, but it proved to be a very resilient organ. Since then, she had built up the belief that no man was so much better than the rest to be worth shedding tears over when they parted. With that philosophy—even though she would not have used such a word to express it—

she took life as it came and no longer grew starry-eyed when somebody showed appreciation of her charms.

Last night had been swell, the girl was willing to admit, but she did not believe it made her a potential Mrs. Mark Counter. Once they reached Elkhorn, which she had discovered was also his destination, they would conclude their respective affairs and go their separate ways. Although she had never heard the word and would not have understood its meaning if she did, she felt sure their destinies lay in different directions. The previous night had been a most enjoyable experience and one she would not soon forget, but nothing serious was going to emerge out of it. However, she hoped their paths would cross in the future and under circumstances which would allow them to renew their acquaintance in a similar fashion.

While Calamity was cooking breakfast, Mark used some of the contents from her water-butt for a wash and shave. Then they ate their food with a very good appetite and made their preparations for continuing the journey. After saddling his bloodbay, he helped her to hitch up the two horses. When all was done and the fire completely extinguished, he swung into the saddle and she boarded the box of the wagon. With a yell and a pop from the long lash of her bullwhip, she set the vehicle moving.

"How come Cap'n Fog's not along with you, Mark?" the girl inquired, as the Texan rode alongside the wagon on the trail he had been following the previous evening and towards which she was making when the accident occurred.

"There was a get-together of trail bosses and cattle buyers in Newton that he had to attend," the blond giant answered. "So, when he got word that a friend of Ole Devil who's ranching out by Elkhorn wants to talk a deal, he asked me to come and do it."

"I'd surely admire to meet Cap'n Fog," Calamity asserted, knowing "Ole Devil" was General Jackson Baines "Ole Devil" Hardin, C.S.A. Rtd., owner of the OD Connected ranch and a very prominent figure in the affairs of Texas despite having been crippled in a riding accident and confined to a wheelchair.[4] "Hey though, how come you went to Newton and not Hays like you did last year?"

4. *New readers, see:* Footnote 8, APPENDIX TWO. *J.T.E.*

"We saved close to a week's driving, way we came north," Mark explained. "Why, did you figure Wild Bill had scared us off?"

"Like I said last night," the girl grinned. "Who's Wild Bill?"

"That's what you said, I'll admit."

"Is all I hear about Cap'n Fog true?"

"Such as?"

"How he stands taller than you, is even stronger and faster'n anybody else with his guns?"

"There's a feller called Doc Leroy who rides for the Wedge can just shade him with one gun," Mark replied. "But I've never come across *anybody* who can using a brace."[5]

"How about the rest of it?" Calamity wanted to know.

"Would you-all believe me was I to tell you Dusty stands no more than five foot six at most?"

"Nope—Hey, you're not jobbing me. You're serious, aren't you."

"It's the living truth, gal," Mark stated. "But, to my way of thinking and to 'most everybody else who meets him, you don't measure Dusty Fog in feet and inches. Comes the chips going down and trouble on its way, he stands the tallest man around."

The time was not too far ahead when Calamity would be able to verify the truth of the blond giant's assertion.

For a time, the girl and her companion discussed Dusty Fog, the Ysabel Kid and other prominent members of the OD Connected ranch's floating outfit. Then she swung the conversation to an item of news which had aroused considerable interest over the past month.

"Have you heard anything more about that hold up Belle Starr and her gang tried to pull down in Wichita?"

"Belle Starr and her gang my ass-hole!" Mark snorted derisively. "Just because somebody reckons there was a woman holding the horses, that doesn't mean it was Belle Starr."

"So you don't reckon it was her?"

"Since when did *Belle Starr* take to robbing banks, or anything else, at gun point?"

"I've never heard tell of it afore myself," Calamity admit-

---

5. *Proof of Mark Counter's assertion can be found in:* GUN WIZARD. *J.T.E.*

ted. "But the bank's offering a thousand dollars to get her brought in alive on dodgers I've seen scattered around 'n' about."

"Much good *that* will do them," Mark sniffed. "She's not mixed up in it, or I'll start to vote Republican."

"I feel a mite sorry for her then," the girl declared. "Way I hear it, the sheriff and his posse run down the four fellers's did the hold up and shot them all to doll rags. Which come out to be more than a mite unfortunate, seeing's they didn't have a thin dime of the money that was took with them and was all too dead to be able to say where it'd gone. So there'll be plenty who reckon's she's got it, or knows where it is, and'll be looking for her to ask."

"It could be and likely will," Mark agreed. "Which, from all I've heard, there's a gal who can take care of herself."

"Yep," Calamity agreed. "I'd sort of like to run across her myself."

"I never took you for a bounty hunter, Calam," the big blond commented, a hint of disapproval in his voice.

"And I god-damned aren't one!" the girl protested indignantly. "It's just that they do say she's a pretty tough gal and I'd admire to find out if it's true."

"From Missouri, huh?" Mark suggested with a grin.

"*Huh*?" Calamity replied, putting the world of puzzlement into the grunt.

"You've got to be shown," the blond giant elaborated.

"I've never yet met the gal's could better me at riding, drinking, cussing, shooting, nor going at it tooth 'n' claw," the red head declared, trying to sound modest without any great success. "And I don't conclude I *ever* will."

Neither Calamity nor Mark realized that, on their next meeting, she would meet a woman who proved to be more than her match in every point she had mentioned.[6]

"So you're not interested in getting your hands on the reward the bank's offering for her?"

"The hell I am. Anybody's can get money out of a son-of-a-bitching *banker* deserves to keep it. Top of which, I go

6. *Told in:* Part One, "Better Than Calamity," THE WILDCATS *and, expanded to include new facts which have been given to us recently,* CUT ONE, THEY ALL BLEED. *J.T.E.*

along with you. I know Sheriff Tamper down to Wichita. He couldn't catch water was he to stand under a waterfall with his hat off. There'd've been no chance of him getting those jaspers like he did had they had Belle Starr running things for them, all I've heard about her."

"What brings you-all out this ways, Calam?" the blond giant inquired, the issue having been overlooked the previous evening.

"I've been delivering a rancher's supplies and'm headed for Elkhorn to see if I can pick up a load to take back with me," the girl replied. "What's it like there? I've never had call to go in afore."

"Nor me," Mark admitted. "But they do say it's booming, growing big, fast and rich what with miners, ranchers and all."

"Are you fixing to be there long?" Calamity asked.

"Day, couple of days at the most," the big blond answered. "Depends on how soon I can see that feller for Ole Devil."

"Could be I'll see you afore I start back then," the girl suggested enthusiastically. "Should it come, we'll have us a whingding and tree the town a mite."

CHAPTER ELEVEN

What Brings *Him* to Elkhorn?

As Mark Counter had informed Calamity Jane, Elkhorn, Montana, was growing big and showed signs of its prosperity. From being a hamlet of not more than two dozen buildings less than nine months earlier, it now supported no less than six thriving saloons. One of them, the Crystal Palace, would not have been out of place in the best part of any major city east, or west, of the Mississippi River. One excellent, one good and two passable hotels catered for the accommodation of transient visitors. Various shops which would usually be under the single roof of a general store in smaller, less lucratively supported towns, could be found on Beidler Street, which was named in honour of John X. Beidler, leader of the vigilantes who wiped out the Plummer gang and ended its depredations in the vicinity of Bannack. Wells Fargo & Company maintained a large combination depot for stage coaches, freight and a telegraph office, testifying to the town's importance.

All the other amenities exhibited a similarly high standard. A stout brick building housed the county offices, court, sheriff's and town marshal's departments and a substantial jail. In addition, Elkhorn offered the usual assortment of livery barns, an undertaker's shop, a bath house, a pool hall and everything else which made life worth living on the range.

Bringing his bloodbay stallion to a halt before the open double doors of a large building above which was a board inscribed, "POP LARKIN'S ORIGINAL AND FIRST ELK-HORN LIVERY BARN Use It, I'm Too Old And Idle To Start Working," the blond giant looked at the red head. Winking, he raised his hat and bowed low over the low horn of his double girthed Texas saddle.[1]

"Don't you forget now!" the girl called, waving her left hand and keeping the wagon moving. "You 'n' me've got us a date when I come back!"

"I wouldn't miss it for the world!" Mark asserted.

Swinging from the saddle, the blond giant watched the girl's vehicle continuing along the street. She had called at the Wells Fargo office in passing, to find a message from her employer ordering her to pick up some equipment from a mine to the west of the town and deliver it to another where it was needed. In view of the urgency and knowing there was a good five more hours of daylight, she had stated her intention of pushing on instead of halting for the night.

Although Mark did not know if he would be in town when Calamity returned, he was tempted to extend his visit and wait for her. His every instinct suggested that proposed celebration would be a most enjoyable experience, more so since he had missed the festivities which followed the delivery and sale of the OD Connected trail herd in Newton due to his volunteering to collect the money owing to Ole Devil Hardin.

Entering the barn with the stallion following on his heels like it was a huge and well trained hound dog, the big Texan found it to his satisfaction. It was cool, light and clean in a fashion which implied it was run by somebody who knew the needs of the horses and was willing to go to trouble to ensure these were met. There were a couple of empty stalls at the end of the right side row and he made his way towards them.

A man had just finished putting up his mount in a stall further along the line. Turning slowly, he looked Mark over. Starting at the gunbelt, then dropping his eyes to take in the high heeled, fancy stitched boots, his gaze roamed upwards to the top of the giant's blond head.

Noticing the way in which the other was staring, Mark was

---

1. *For the benefit of new readers; because "cinch" had Mexican connotations, the majority of Texans employed the word "girth" — generally pronounced "girt" — for the short, broad band made from coarsely woven horsehair, canvas, or cordage and terminated at each end with a metal ring and which, assisted by the latigo, is used to fasten the saddle on the horse's back. As Texans knotted the end of the rope to the saddlehorn when working, instead of using a "dally" which could be slipped free in an emergency, their rigs had two girths for greater security. J.T.E.*

reminded of a rancher studying a prime bull and wondering if it would bring in any profit should he buy it.

For his part, the blond giant returned the scrutiny in a quick and all-embracing glance. He liked nothing of what he saw. Although the other's attire gave little indication of how he earned his living, the two revolvers in the holsters of his gunbelt and the ten gauge shotgun leaning against the gate of the stall suggested they could form a substantial proportion of the means by which his income was derived.

Having completed his examination of the newcomer, the man turned away after the fashion of a rancher who had concluded the animal under observation would be unlikely to prove profitable. Swinging the saddle over his shoulder with his right hand in a way which suggested there was considerable strength in his somewhat scrawny-looking frame, he closed and fastened the gate with his left. Then, picking up the shotgun by the small of the butt and keeping his forefinger alongside the triggerguard, he walked towards the front entrance.

Without appearing to, Mark watched until the man had left the barn. That was what he considered to be a wise precaution under the circumstances. Anybody who behaved in such a manner struck him as being a person to be treated warily.

"Can't say's I'm sorry to see *him* leave, neither."

The comment was uttered by a shortish, plump and amiable looking elderly man who came from the door marked, "Office," at the left side of the building. His accent was as indicative of birth in Texas as that of the blond giant.

"I've seen folks's I'd rather ride the river with," Mark admitted.

"You-all know him?" the newcomer inquired.

"Nope. Should I?"

"Not less'n you've got a wanted dodger on ye some place or other. And you-all don't have, or likely one or t'other of you'd be dead by now. That there was Jubal Framant, young feller."

"It was, huh?"

Despite his apparently laconic acceptance of the information, the blond giant once more swung his gaze in the direction of its subject. Framant was engaged in conversation, with obvious reluctance, at the other side of the street. The other man involved was big, burly, clad in the attire of a working cowhand; but with the badge of a town marshal pinned to his calfskin vest and a Colt Model of 1848 Dragoon revolver holstered at his right side. Although some people considered anybody who toted one of the massive, four pounds, one ounce, thumb-busting handguns as old fashioned and out of date, Mark did not subscribe to the view. The Ysabel Kid carried such a weapon and had demonstrated how effective it could be on more than one occasion.

"Yes sir, that's Jubal Framant, sure's I was born," the old timer reiterated. "I wonder what brings *him* to Elkhorn?"

"There's only one thing takes a son-of-a-bitch like him any place," Mark replied, being just as aware of the bounty hunter's reputation as the man he was addressing appeared to be. Framant was said to be one of the worst and most ruthless to follow the ignoble business of seeking out wanted criminals for the rewards which were offered and it was rumored that he had never taken in a living prisoner. "Who-all's the feller talking to him?"

"Joel Stocker, town marshal and a real nice jasper to boot," the old man answered, then turned his attention to the blood-bay and squinted at its flank. "R Over C. Now *that's* a brand I've never seed afore."

"Do tell."

"Ask anybody, 'cepting them's's jealous, and they'll tell you's how Pop Larkin knows ever danged brand within five hundred miles."

"Could be the R Over C's five hundred and *one* miles away, though," the blond giant pointed out, having guessed the other's identity.

"Should that be how close she be," the old timer chuckled, "somebody's sneaked South Texas a hell of a way's north. 'Less I miss my guess, it's Big Rance Counter's Big Bend spread."

"It's his all right," Mark confirmed.

"Tolerable tallish feller, that Rance Counter, I've heard tell. Likely he'd sire pretty hefty sons."

"I'm the lil baby of the family."

"Mark Counter, huh?" the old man assessed. "Pleased to know you-all. Like you might've guessed, I'm Pop Larkin and I keep this place. Leastwise, it don't keep me."

"You look right poorly done by," the blond giant drawled, leading his horse into one of the empty stalls. "Wonder what Framant wants here."

"I asked you-all *first*," Larkin protested. "And it ain't 'what,' it's '*who*.' I'll fetch some water and grain, happen you need any."

"I'd be obliged if you would," Mark assented.

"Howdy, mister," a gentle voice drawled, as the blond giant was stripping the saddle from his horse.

Looking over his shoulder, Mark concluded that for a big man Marshal Joel Stocker could move very quietly. Leaning on the stall's gate and chewing almost meditatively on a plug of tobacco, there was a deceptive lethargy about the peace officer which might have fooled some people. It failed to achieve this result with the person he had addressed.

"Howdy," the big blond replied, continuing with his work.

"I haven't seen you around these parts afore," Stocker commented. "Or have I?"

"I wouldn't reckon so, marshal, seeing's I've only just now rode in."

"With Calamity Jane?"

"Sure."

"She's Wild Bill Hickok's gal, way I heard it."

"Has *Wild Bill* heard it?" Mark countered.

"Don't reckon it'd scare *you* none, happen he had," Stocker stated, in his sleepy tone. "It'd worry me some, though, me being a duly sworn and appointed officer of the law 'n' duty bound to keep the peace. Which same, I'd's soon not have two gents like you and Wild Bill locking horns in my bailiwick."

"If Wild Bill's anywheres near here, I've not heard tell of it," Mark declared. "Calam and me met up on the trail is all, I haven't snuck her away from him, but I'll likely see her tomorrow if she gets back from the chore she's headed to handle."

"Mind if I ask what's fetched you here?" the marshal inquired, but the words were clearly a demand for information employed in a way which should offer no offence.

"I've come to see Tom Gamble," the blond giant answered, having served as a peace officer and being aware that his interrogator was merely taking a sensible precaution in the line of duty.

The faint air of watchful suspicion left Stocker's face. Straightening up, he raised his eyes to meet those of Mark—something he *very* rarely found need to do with any man—and extended his right hand.

"Sorry, friend," the marshal apologised. "Reckon having Framant come to town's got me a mite edgy. Are you Cap'n Fog?"

"Mark Counter," the big blond corrected.

"Whooee!" Stocker ejaculated, running an appraising gaze over the other. "Happen Cap'n Fog's got more heft than *you*, he must be a tolerable sizeable gent."

Feeling no resentment, Mark allowed the comment to pass. It had been several years since he had last been surprised that anybody should mistake him for his *amigo*, or persist in believing Dusty was a larger man than was the case. What was more, he realized that he had the physical appearance many people expected of a man with the small Texan's legendary reputation. The erroneous conclusion was something they had turned to their advantage in the past and would continue to do so when the occasion demanded.[2]

"Do you allus look over visitors like this?" the blond giant asked amiably.

"Find it makes life a whole slew easier to have a notion of who-all's in town and why," Stocker answered. "And I'm a man who allus likes to make life easier for me, which there's some less welcome here than others."

"Like that bounty hunting son-of-a-bitch, Framant, heh, Joel?" suggested Larkin, approaching with a pail of water and sack of grain. "Have you-all told him to haul his ass out of town?"

"Nope," the marshal replied. "I ain't saying I'm not doing it 'cause he scares me, even if he do a mite. But he's got his rights under the Constitution of these here United States—and *knows* 'em. Like he said, I can't run a man out of town just 'cause I'm not took with his line of work."

"Got me a burro in the office," Larkin remarked, as the big Texan emerged from the stall at the conclusion of attending to

---

2. *New readers, see:* Footnote 3, APPENDIX TWO. *J.T.E.*

his stallion's immediate needs. "You can leave your rig on it, happen you're so minded."

"*Gracias*, I'll do that," Mark accepted, guessing from the way Stocker glanced from him to the owner of the barn and back that he was being given a privilege not accorded to everybody. "I thought you didn't have one when I saw Framant toting his saddle out with him."

"There's them's get to use it and them's *don't*," Larkin asserted. "Fetch her along this way."

Following the old man, Mark entered the large office and hung his saddle on the inverted V-shaped wooden rack known as a burro. Like any cowhand, he preferred to make use of such a facility should one be available. It offered less chance of having somebody step on the rig than when it was laid upon the ground. Although he took the bedroll from the cantle and drew the Winchester out of the boot, it did not imply a lack of faith in Larkin's honesty. His spare clothing and shaving gear was among the other gear in the war bag wrapped in the roll and nobody with any sense left a loaded rifle where youngsters might have an opportunity to get hold of it.

"Which's the best hotel in town?" the blond giant inquired, joining Stocker at the front entrance after having paid for the stabling and keep of his stallion.

"Ryan's Bella Union down there, right next to the Crystal Palace," the marshal replied, pointing along the street. "Say though, Tom bust his leg coming off a bad one. He sent word in that somebody from the OD Connected'd be dropping by and to send whoever it was out to see him."

"How far out is it?"

"Two, three hours steady ride. Only you couldn't make it by nightfall now you've fed your hoss."

"I'll leave it until morning, he could use the rest," Mark decided. "What's the Crystal Palace like, speaking as a duly appointed officer of the law, that is."

"Well run and fair," Stocker declared. "Got some real pretty gals there and you'll walk out with any money you don't spend—or lose trying to beat the blackjack dealer."

"My momma told me never to buck the dealer's percentage at *any* game, especially blackjack."

"It's not the *game* you'll go to buck in there. It's the dealer."

"What makes him so special?"

"Being a *her*," grinned Stocker. "And a right pretty one at that. Was I not a married man, which I'm *not*, I'd sure admire to stake a few myself on beating her game."

"She's as good as that, huh?" Mark drawled, ignoring the somewhat ambiguous way in which the peace officer's explanation was worded.

"*Better*," Stocker corrected. "Although she's not the kind you'd expect to find dealing blackjack, even in a place as decent and well run as the Palace."

"They never are," Mark said with a touch of cynicism. "See you, marshal."

"I'm likely to be around," Stocker said, and conveying the impression that he was about to fall asleep on his feet, he slouched away.

Possessing an excellent judgement where such matters were concerned, Mark Counter decided that the marshal had greatly understated when describing the lady blackjack dealer at the Crystal Palace as "a right pretty one at that." In his own estimation, she was the most attractive woman he had ever seen. A radiantly beautiful young blonde, she was clad in a white satin gown more suitable to a formal ball in a Southern States' mansion than a Western town and it showed off the contours of a magnificent figure to their best advantage without being openly blatant.

Having taken a room at the Bella Union Hotel, the blond giant had waited until nine o'clock before setting out to discover what Elkhorn had to offer. He had spent the intervening period, as the majority of cowhands did when visiting a town with money in their pockets,[3] by calling at the nearby barber's shop and availing himself of the various facilities it offered. He had had a haircut, a shave, a long soak in a hot bath and

3. *The author suspects that the trend in film and television Westerns made since the early 1960's to portray all cowhands as long haired and filthy has arisen less from the production companies' desire to create "realism" than because there were so few supporting players with short hair. In our extensive reference library, we cannot find a dozen photographs of cowhands—as opposed to mountain men, Army scouts, or prospectors—with long hair and bushy beards. In fact, our reading on the subject has led us to assume the term "long hair" was one of derision and opprobrium in the cattle country of the Old West as it is to this day. J.T.E.*

had a shine put on his boots. Then, having changed into fresh clothing in his room and eaten an excellent meal, he decided to follow Stocker's advice with regards to the establishment which would be at least the starting point for evening's relaxation.

Despite his conclusions, Mark did not attempt to join the blackjack game at that moment. Such was the attraction of the dealer, it would have been almost impossible to find a place at the table. Like the other customers in the well filled bar-room, the players represented a cross-section of the region's population. There were cowhands, mine workers, town dwellers of differing grades of affluence, soldiers, professional gamblers and even men whose attire proclaimed them to be French-canadians or *Metis* from north of the nearby international border. All seemed to be on amiable terms, with no sign of the tensions and hostilities which occasionally existed between such diverse factions and sometimes conflicting business interests.

A long wooden board, nailed to the wall just to the side of the blackjack table, caught the blond giant's eye as he was making for the bar. Strolling over, he looked at the reward posters which were thumb-tacked to it. The "dodger" given pride of place in the centre drew of his attention.

WANTED
$1,000 REWARD
ALIVE ONLY
BELLE STARR

Beneath the proclamation was a sketch of a beautiful, if hard-faced woman with shoulder length black hair, who had a black Stetson on the back of her head and a triple strand pearl necklace encircling her throat. Reading the description under the illustration—height, about six foot; build, Junoesque; age, late thirties; heavily bejewelled and made-up with rouge—Mark wondered if it was accurate. To the best of his knowledge, the lady outlaw had never been captured to be measured and sketched. While not yet as extensive as they would become,[4] his experiences as a peace officer had given him a

---

4. *Details of Mark Counter's career as a peace officer before and after the events recorded in this volume are given in:* QUIET TOWN, THE MAKING OF A LAWMAN, THE TROUBLE BUSTERS, THE GENTLE GIANT, THE SMALL TEXAN *and* THE TOWN TAMERS. *J.T.E.*

hearty scepticism where the accuracy of the average witness to a crime was concerned. He knew that, all too often, imagination was allowed to take over if facts were blurred.

However, the blond giant's thoughts on the subject were diverted by seeing that somebody had written in large red letters between the name and the sketch, "THE TOUGHEST GAL IN THE WEST." A grin came to his face as he wondered what Calamity Jane would say when or if she read the addition.

CHAPTER TWELVE

Doesn't That Sound *Forward* of Me

Instincts which had grown acute through years of living dangerously warned Mark Counter he was being watched by unfriendly eyes from two different points not too far away. Turning away from the board, he glanced about him as if doing nothing more than casually examining his surroundings. He had no difficulty in deciding from where the disturbing scrutinies were originating.

Jubal Framant was standing alone at the counter, but dropped his gaze to the glass of beer he was holding as the blond giant's gaze reached him. Noticing that the shotgun was leaning at his right side, Mark wondered if he always carried it with him.

However, the big Texan did not ponder for long about the bounty hunter's armament. The other watcher appeared to be the largest of four unshaven, gun-hung men at a nearby table. While they wore clothing which suggested they were cowhands, Mark doubted whether any of them had ever worked cattle and was willing to bet that, if they had, it would not have been on behalf of the owner. Realizing he could have made his curiosity apparent, the man started talking with his companions.

Strolling towards an open space at the bar, some distance from Framant's position, Mark wondered what had aroused the interest in him. He did not attribute it to admiration for his manly figure. He concluded the same idea might be in both the observers' minds, that he was a bounty hunter and looking to see if any new rewards were being offered; or the member of the quartet could be considering him as the possible victim of a robbery.

Deciding he would be able to cope with the latter contingency should it arise, which would not be while he was in the Crystal Palace Saloon, the blond giant ordered a beer. Receiving it, he turned his attention once more to the blackjack table. He saw the beautiful blonde dealer was rising. Her place was taken by one of the male employees who had been helping her and, giving the players a dazzling smile accompanied by the assurance that she would return later, she walked away. She was making for where a door led into the alley between the saloon and the Bella Union Hotel and a flight of stairs gave access to the upper floor of the building.

Glancing at the four hard-cases, Mark saw they too were watching the blonde. One of them started to rise, but the largest growled a *sotto voce* order which caused him to sit down again as she went past the door and ascended the stairs.

Interest in the blackjack game waned with the blonde's departure. The swarm of players and kibitzers faded away, leaving only a handful of devotees around the table. Making the most of the opportunity, the big Texan carried his schooner of beer over and acquired one of the vacant chairs.

"No offence, friend," the relief dealer said amiably, waiting for Mark to buy chips. "But I'd've taken you for a poker player."

"None took and I am usually," the blond giant replied with a grin. "But you've such a good and kindly face, I figured you-all would take pity on a poor stranger and let me win."

"Well I'll swan!" the dealer countered. "And there I was thinking you'd come over to make sure you'd have a seat when Miss Marigold gets back."

"Miss Marigold?" Mark prompted.

"Miss Marigold Tremayne," the saloon worker explained. "The lady whose place I'm taking for a spell."

"Was there a lady here?" the big blond inquired innocently. "I didn't notice."

"You sure you can see well enough to play?" the dealer challenged.

"Toss me a card or so and I'll find out," Mark suggested. "Which I do sort of recollect seeing there was a lady dealing, but I hardly gave her a glance."

"You sure you're *alive* enough to play?" the dealer asked, starting to do as he had been requested.

The lady dealer returned after the blond giant had been playing for something over half an hour. Coming to his feet, he removed his Stetson and made a courtly bow. Acknowledging it with a graceful inclination of her torso, she spoke in the accent of a well bred Southron.

"Good evening, sir. You're a Texan, I see."

"Yes, ma'am, Miss Tremayne. I was born in the Big Bend country, but I'm riding for the OD Connected these days. My name's Mark Counter."

"I've heard of the OD Connected and, of course, of you-all, Mr. Counter," the blonde declared, then waved her left hand towards the other men who were gathering hurriedly. "Please be seated, sir. Although I doubt whether *anybody* would be so indiscreet as to try to take *your* chair."

Watching the way in which Marigold Tremayne's hands flipped out the cards when the game was resumed, Mark could detect nothing to suggest she employed her beauty and charm as a cover for some form of cheating. Her fingers were devoid of rings which might have had a tiny mirror attached as an aid to discovering the value of each card as it was being dealt, or a spike used for marking the deck during the play. Nor were her nails long enough to achieve a similar result. She had placed her somewhat large white satin reticule on the table near her right hand, but its neck was fastened by the combined draw- and carrying-string.

Two hours slipped by most enjoyably and with what seemed to have been remarkable rapidity for the blond giant. Due to a series of losing hands having caused his original stake to be deplete, he stood up and took out his wallet. Extracting a couple of ten dollar bills, he passed them, with a request for more chips, across the table to the man who had been relief dealer. As he was starting to sit down, after having returned the wallet to his back pocket, a plump brunette saloongirl stepped from among the small crowd of kibitzers.

"Let me give you a hug for luck, big feller," the girl suggested, slipping her left arm around Mark's shoulders and leaning against him.

Removing the arm, the brunette stepped away and the blond giant began to turn, opening his mouth. Before he could speak, an icy feminine voice—which had lost its previous suggestion of blooming magnolias, mint juleps on the lawn of a Deep South mansion and coloured folks singing plaintive songs—beat him to it.

"Give it back to the gentleman, Lily!"

"Give *what* back?" the brunette demanded, stepping clear of the crowd and glaring angrily at the speaker.

"The gentleman's wallet!" Marigold answered, having risen, walking around the table until she was confronting the saloongirl. "Hand it over and stay well away from my game in future."

"Yeah?" Lily sneered, starting to raise her hands and curving the long-nailed fingers like claws. "And who's going to make m——?"

Without giving the slightest warning of what she intended to do, Marigold folded her right hand into a fist. Swinging it with a masculine precision, she sent the knuckles under the brunette's jaw. Caught unawares, Lily was lifted on to her toes and went down to land in a sitting position. Bending, the blonde grasped her by the ankles and lifted until she looked as if she was standing on her head. Amid laughter from the on-lookers—including the other girls, Mark noticed—Marigold giggled her captive until his wallet slid from the bosom of the garish dress. Releasing her hold and allowing Lily to collapse on to the floor, the blonde picked up and returned his property.

"I apologise for this, sir," Marigold said. "The owner and floor manager don't allow the girls to do such things, sir," Marigold said," but Lily only started this afternoon and that doesn't appear to have sunk into her head yet."

"I felt it go," the big blond replied, pushing the wallet into his pocket once more. "But I don't think I could've got it back as easily as you-all."

"The feminine touch can work wonders," Marigold smiled, her voice resuming the timbre it had had prior to addressing the errant saloongirl. "Shall we continue the game? I go off in half an hour."

"It'll be my pleasure, ma'am," Mark asserted and sat down.

At the end of the half an hour, the blonde folded the cards and handed them to the relief dealer. Standing up, she waved aside the objections from various players to her departure.

"Why gentlemen," Marigold said, directing a dazzling

smile around the table. "You wouldn't want a lady to miss her beauty sleep, now would you-all?"

Studying the way the other players looked at the blonde, Mark felt sure they would have willingly stood guard around wherever she was living to make sure nobody disturbed her rest if she had asked them.

Leaving her assistants to cash in the chips and disband the game, Marigold walked majestically across the room and up the stairs. Having received the money due to him, a change in his fortunes bringing back most of his earlier losses, Mark stood and glanced around. Framant had left the bar, but was sitting alone at a table with the shotgun laid in front of him across it. The sight of him caused the blond giant to remember and look for the four hard-cases. They had left their table and Mark could see no sign of them anywhere else in the room. However, as he was on the point of dismissing them from his thoughts, he noticed the biggest standing on the sidewalk and watching the inside of the saloon.

For a moment, the big blond wondered if he was the subject of the hard-case's scrutiny. Then he realized the watcher was not looking at him even overtly, but had the stairs up which Marigold had disappeared under observation. Fifteen minutes went by, with the man remaining on the sidewalk and Mark maintaining his surveillance via the mirror behind the bar. Then the other stiffened and turned to walk away. Flickering a glance across the room, Mark saw the blonde was descending from the upper floor. She was now wearing a wide brimmed, fancy hat, had a white shawl draped across her shoulders and the reticule dangled by its carrying straps from her left wrist. Waving her right hand in acknowledgement of the calls of, "Good night, Miss Marigold," which came from all sides, she made her way to the side door.

Remembering the way in which a member of the quartet had behaved earlier, the blond giant revised his opinion. Up until that moment, he had thought Marigold had living quarters upstairs. Now he decided this might not be the case. Or, if she did, she had the habit of going off the premises for a meal at the conclusion of the night's work. Finishing his glass of beer, he put down the glass and strode swiftly towards the front doors. By the time he reached the sidewalk, the hard-case was no longer in sight and he turned in the appropriate direction to confirm his suspicions.

A muffled gasp, a startled exclamation, a thud and an angry, pain-filled yelp came to Mark's ears as he was approaching the alley which separated the saloon from the hotel. Turning the corner, there was sufficient light for him to see what was happening. Two of the hard-cases were gripping the blonde by the arms and trying to drag her to the rear of the building. Mouthing profanities, the third was hopping on one leg and holding the other shin.

Although that accounted for three of the quartet, the largest of them was missing!

Sensing rather than seeing the last of the four, Mark made a fast side-step and twisting his body, he ducked his head forward, hearing the hiss as something passed behind him. The impetus with which the abortive blow from the butt of the Colt was delivered caused his assailant to stumble forward to the accompaniment of a startled imprecation. Driving his elbow to the rear, the blond giant felt it impact against the approaching man's *solar plexus*. Feeling as if he had been kicked by a mule, the recipient's words changed into an agonized gurgle and he reeled backwards even more swiftly than he had advanced.

Seeing that Mark had avoided the attack, had dealt with his companion, and was advancing, the third hard-case released the leg kicked by Marigold. Lunging forward, he rammed his head into the big blond's torso. Despite grunting, Mark withstood the impact and, bending swiftly, locked his arms around his attacker's body from above. Straightening up, he hoisted his captive into the air with no more discernible effort than as if he was handling a baby. Holding the man across his right shoulder, he swung around and released his grip. Propelled through the air, the man crashed into the wall of the saloon and bounced limply from it to the ground.

A hand caught the blond giant's left shoulder from behind and he was swung around. Having been less severely hurt than he had imagined, the largest of the quartet had returned to the fray. Coming around, the other fist smashed against the side of Mark's jaw, sending him reeling against the wall of the hotel. Hitting it with his shoulders, he wondered why Marigold was keeping so quiet. By all rules of feminine conduct, she ought to be screeching for help at the top of her voice. Yet, apart from the first startled gasp and the hissing of her breath as she struggled in the grasp of her captors, she was making no sound.

There was no time for the blond giant to ponder upon the blonde's untypical behaviour. Instead, having been prevented from falling by reaching the wall, he thrust himself forward to meet the continuation of the fourth man's attack. While the other threw a good punch, he lacked science and relied upon brute force. Which was not the best means to employ when dealing with Mark Counter.

Bringing up his right hand, the big blond deflected the wild blow from his attacker over his shoulder. At almost the same instant, his left fist flew to strike the point upon which his elbow had landed, but with far greater force. As the man gave a strangled squawk and folded over, Mark's right rose like iron filings drawn by a magnet and met the descending jaw. Lifted erect, the hard-case was in no condition to avoid the left cross with which his assailant followed up the other blows.

"Look out!" Marigold shouted, as the blond giant's punch pitched its recipient on a collision course with the wall of the saloon.

Glancing over his shoulder, Mark found that the blonde was now held by only one of her captors. He was grasping her from behind by both arms and, reaching for a gun, his companion was moving forward. However, she did not merely restrict herself to warning her rescuer of the danger. Bringing up her right foot, she placed it on the rump of the man in front of her and, before she could be stopped, shoved. Taken unawares by the action and the strength with which it was carried out, he was hurriedly sent forward and the revolver fell from his hand. Nor were his troubles over. Swinging to meet him, Mark lashed out a power packed blow which precipitated him in an unconcious heap on top of the previous victim of similar treatment.

Having felled his latest intended assailant, the blond giant gave his attention to the girl. He found that she was already taking care of herself. Bringing down her leg from the shove, she sent it behind her. Nor was it the instinctive reaction of a terrified member of the "weaker sex," but a calculated move which allowed her to rake the sole of her shoe down her captor's shin. Yelping in pain, he relaxed his hold sufficiently for her to break free of it. Nor did she restrict herself to just the liberation. Swiveling around, she drove up her left knee to where it would prove most efficacious.

Instantly, the man's agonized profanity ended in a squawk of sheer torment. Clutching the point of impact, he began to bend at the waist. Grasping the reticule in both hands, Marigold swung it after the fashion of the batter in a baseball game. Watching and listening as he was advancing to her assistance, Mark thought the thud of the reticule's meeting with the man's jaw sounded remarkably solid. Nor did his point of view change as the last of the quartet made an almost graceful pirouette before joining the others in an unconcious sprawl to the ground.

Light flooded into the alley as the side door of the saloon flew open. The floor manager and two of the bouncers burst out, skidding to a halt and staring at the sight which confronted them.

"What the—?" the manager began.

"It's all right, Mr. Cahill," Marigold replied, bending over to retrieve the shawl which had slipped from her shoulders and, on straightening up, adjusting her hat to its previous position. "These—gentlemen—must have been drinking more than is wise and it made them a trifle impulsive."

"Did they, by god!" the manager growled. "Do you want me to send for Joel Stocker and have them tossed in the pokey?"

"I hardly think that's necessary," the blonde refused. "I'm sure they've learned their lesson and won't do anything of the sort again. Take them around the back and revive them, then send them on their way."

"Sure, if that's the way *you* want it," the manager assented, then nodded to the bouncers. "Do you want the boys to see you to the hotel?"

"I'm going there myself," Mark commented. "May I have the honour of escorting you-all, ma'am?"

"Why thank you, Mr. Counter," Marigold replied, dipping a slight curtsy. "I'm most grateful for your kind offer."

Offering the big Texan her arm, the blonde said her goodnights to the three men from the saloon. Remarking that she always used the rear entrance as they set off, she guided him in the appropriate direction. While walking along, she suggested they had supper together. They did so, talking about general matters as they were eating. Marigold showed no interest in his personal affairs and he refrained from asking about hers. At the conclusion of the meal, he accompanied her upstairs. However, although their rooms were at opposite ends of the corridor, she made no attempt to release his arm and pulled gently to the right.

"I do declare the excitement has been too much for me to go to sleep yet," the blonde remarked. "I—I don't suppose you would care to come to my room and talk for a while, would you, Mr. Counter—?" Then her right hand fluttered to her lips and she dropped her gaze demurely to the floor before going on, "Land's sakes a-mercy. Doesn't that sound *forward* of me? I realize I should *never* have invited you unchaperoned to my room—Nor would I, but you are a *Southern* gentleman, aren't you?"

"I try to be, ma'am," Mark replied. "And I'd be honoured to accept."

Leading the way and unlocking the door, Marigold allowed the blond giant to precede her into the room. Crossing to the dressing table, he turned up the wick of the lamp and glanced around. As he was deciding the furnishings were little different from those of his own quarters, he heard the click of the lock and looked to where his hostess was turning from the door.

"It blows open unless I keep it locked," Marigold explained, walking forward, the demure expression and innocence of her tone at odds with the look in her eyes. "Now, in what way can I entertain you-all?"

Despite having a few ideas on the subject, Mark kept them to himself. Although he was puzzled by the blonde's actions, he decided to go along with her for a time. He was aware that he could be the intended victim of a "badger" game, where an irate "husband" or "fiance" would burst in demanding restitution for the "alienation of her affections," but doubted whether this would be the case. Unless he was mistaken, she was far too intelligent to consider he would be a profitable victim.

"I know," Marigold said, going to the sidepiece and, having placed her reticule on it, opening the middle drawer. "Put a chair on either side of the bed and then you can teach me to play *poker*."

"Why sure," the blond giant assented, showing nothing of his suspicions.

By the time Mark had carried out his instructions, the blonde was holding a deck of cards she had taken from the drawer. Coming over as he sat down, she took the chair at the other side of the bed. Neither removing her hat and shawl, nor shuffling and offering the cards to be cut, she started to deal. Knowing that she possessed sufficient knowledge of gambling to be unlikely to forget two such basic and important conventions, Mark decided against raising a comment. Instead, he kept quiet and waited to see what the next development would be.

Picking up the five cards which were dealt to him, the big blond fanned them out as Marigold was placing the remainder of the deck between them and collecting her own hand. Good poker player though he was, he could not prevent himself blinking at what he saw. They were the ace, king, queen, jack and ten of hearts. Studying the cards, he was even more puzzled. Three possibilities suggested themselves to him. First, she had made a mistake and dealt him the hand intended for herself from the "cold deck." Second, the deal was fair and the straight flush had come out, as it might be expected to do once in 649,740 hands. Third, she had deliberately given him an unbeatable hand for some purpose of her own which he could not imagine. Only if there were jokers, or "wild" cards in play would it be possible—by holding four of a kind and the joker, or a "wild" card—could she attain better than a stand off against his royal straight flush. He could see the jokers in the open box and, unless so stipulated, "wild" cards were not permitted.

"What stakes are we playing for?" Mark inquired, watching the beautiful face.

"Good heavens!" Marigold gasped, looking horrified. "You-all surely don't think I would play cards for *money* with a *gentleman* while we are *alone*?"

"I apologise for being so thoughtless, ma'am," Mark replied, still unable to decide what was intended.

"And I accept," the blonde replied. "But 'ma'am' sounds so *formal*. I think, under the circumstances, you might call me 'Marigold' if I may be permitted to address you-all as 'Mark.'"

"I reckon we've known each other long enough for *that*," the blond giant assented. "What now, *Marigold*?"

"Just for *fun*, I'll open with my hat," the blonde replied, glancing at her cards and removing her headdress to drop it over the foot of the bed. Lifting her eyes to meet Mark's speculative gaze, she went on with a hint of almost guileless challenge in her voice. "That's not like playing for money, now *is* it?"

"It's not the same thing at all," Mark confirmed, taking his hat from where he had hung it on the back of the chair. "I'll see yours and raise my bandana."

"Are we playing *table* stakes?" Marigold inquired coyly.

"It's the *only* way to play."

"Hum! My shawl to cover the bandana and—!"

Raising first one and then the other foot on to the bed, the blonde removed the shoes and black stockings from as shapely a pair of legs as Mark had seen—well, since early that morning.

"My shoes and stockings to raise," Marigold offered and continued in a faintly chiding fashion. "But a *gentleman* would have looked away."

"I would have, but my momma always taught me never to look away from the table when I'm playing poker," Mark answered, drawing off his boots. "And you-all wouldn't have wanted me to go against momma's advice, now would you?"

"I should think *not*, for shame!" Marigold declared.

The raising and re-raising continued for a few more rounds. At last, Marigold looked downwards and then over the foot of the bed.

"Why I do declare! I haven't another thing with which to raise—unless I go to the wardrobe and—."

"Huh huh!" Mark objected. "When you-all play table stakes, you bet just what you've brought to the table with you."

"Then, as *neither* of us has anything left with which to bet, what can we do?"

"Turn our hands over and have a showdown."

Delivering the ruling, Mark carried it out. After staring for a moment, Marigold gave what sounded like a gasp of innocent surprise and turned over her cards. They proved to be the ace, king, queen, jack and ten of diamonds.

"Heavens to Betsy, we've *both* got the same value hand!"

"It sure looks that way!" Mark agreed, reaching out to turn down the lamp's flame.

"You know, Mark," the blonde said in hardly more than a whisper, her chair scraping back. "There are actually men who would take advantage of a poor defenceless girl at a time like this."

"The dirty dogs!" the blond giant answered, sensing rather than seeing or hearing the girl as she came around the bed. Her hand found his, tugging at it with gentle insistence. "But no Southern gentleman would think of doing such a thing."

"What's this swelling on your neck?" Marigold inquired, after several minutes in which the only sounds had not been human conversation.

"Something bit me," the blond giant replied.

Silence descended for a moment, then the blonde said gently, "You mean like *this*?"

CHAPTER THIRTEEN

She's Belle Starr

"Dearie me," Marigold Tremayne purred, lying in bed with half of her naked body uncovered and watching Mark Counter as he ran a finger gingerly over the oval swelling on the left side of his neck. "Did I do *that*?"

"If you *didn't*," the blond giant replied, turning from the mirror of the sidepiece, "there must have been somebody else in here last night."

"Good heavens!" the blonde gasped, staring about her in well simulated alarm. "Perhaps you'd best come back and help me make sure there still *isn't*."

"Well now," Mark drawled. "I've got to go out to the Gamble place this morning—!"

"May I come along?" Marigold requested, showing eagerness. "We could hire a surrey and take along a picnic basket."

"Now there's a right smart notion," Mark declared. "I'll go see if Pop Larkin has one right after breakfast and you can fix up with the kitchen here for the basket."

"That's just what I was going to suggest," Marigold conceded, but pulled back the covers and patted the bed by her side. "Only my momma always told me one should never rush into *anything* early in the morning and you-all wouldn't want to prove her wrong, now *would* you?"

"It wouldn't be the gentlemanly thing to do," the blond giant asserted and returned to climb into bed.

"Who bit you?" Marigold inquired, half an hour later, as Mark was donning sufficient clothing to return to his room so he could wash and shave.

"You did."

"I meant *first*."

"Calamity Jane."

"You're funning me!" Marigold stated, but her smile died and was replaced by a frown as she studied the big Texan's face and she shook her head. "No, you're *not*. Calamity Jane really *did* bite you."

"Why sure," Mark confirmed. "She's quite a gal. Came through town yesterday and's likely to be back tonight."

"Is she?" the blonde sniffed.

Although Marigold's attitude implied that the matter was closed as far as she was concerned, the blond giant decided it might be advisable to prevent her from meeting Calamity Jane.

Walking towards the livery barn, Mark Counter was surprised when the town marshal came out of it and started to go by without either speaking or appearing to notice him.

"She must be quite a gal," the blond giant remarked.

"Huh?" Joel Stocker grunted, coming to a halt and grinning sheepishly. "Sorry, Mark, I was thinking."

"It surely looked that way, *amigo*. And when a feller's thinking that thoughtful, there's usually a right pretty gal at the end of it."

"For you danged Texas Johnny Rebs, maybe, but us fellers up here in Montana allus take life more serious."

"That being the case," Mark drawled. "How'd you-all ever get around to having any lil fellers here in Montana?"

"We know there's a time and place for everything," Stocker explained, as seriously as if delivering a State secret, then lost the levity. "Right now, I'm thinking about the killing last night."

"Anybody I know?" the blond giant inquired.

"Likely you didn't get 'round to being introduced formal," Stocker answered. "But you had a nodding acquaintance with him earlier—or, maybe a throwing against the wall acquaintance'd be closer to it."

"That went straight by without me being able to draw a bead on it," Mark said in genuine puzzlement.

"He was one of the four yahoos you 'n' Miss Tremayne tangled with in the alley last night," Stocker explained. "I saw it start and was just fixing to bill in when you took cards.

Seemed like you didn't need no help 'cept what she gave, so I didn't spoil your fun."

"Why bless your kind lil old Yankee heart," Mark grinned, then he became serious again. "Who-all did the killing?"

"Framant."

"Was it self defence?"

"Wasn't nothing nor nobody to say it *wasn't*," the marshal said sombrely. "Happened out back of the Black Cat Cafe. Framant allowed he recognized Wicker, same being the name that jasper's wanted under. When he went to bring him in, Wicker grabbed for his gun and died of a case of slow."

"Which isn't surprising, seeing he was stacked up against a scattergun," Mark commented.

"Seems like he *wasn't*," Stocker corrected. "Least, Framant made wolf bait of him with one of those foreign handguns he totes on his belt. Now he stands to pick up the seven hundred and fifty dollars bountys's being offered on Wicker by a sheriff down to the Indian nations line in Kansas."

"Do you reckon he's the reason Framant came here?"

"He reckons he wasn't, but just happened on Wicker by accident."

"They were both down to the Crystal Palace last night."

"I saw them all in there when I looked in," Stocker admitted. "Allowed he wasn't sure it was Wicker until he'd been back to his hotel and checked on the dodgers he totes around, which could be true seeing's he fetched the one on him to show me."

"I never saw *you* in the Palace last night," Mark claimed.

"Which don't surprise me none," Stocker replied. "You was too busy a-drinking and a-carousing. 'Sides which, I'm not nowheres near so pretty as Miss Tremayne."

"You-all won't get an argument from me on *that*," the blond giant stated. "How about those three jaspers who were with Wicker?"

"They've lit a shuck out of town," Stocker answered. "Likely figured Framant'd be gunning for them next. I wonder what they wanted from Miss Tremayne?"

"Maybe reckoned she was carrying her cut from the game and aimed to wideloop it," Mark suggested.

"That could be," the peace officer conceded. "Well, I'm

not like some's I could name and have work to do. Are you fixing to ride out to see Tom Gamble?"

"As soon as I've hired a surrey," Mark confirmed. "I'm taking Marigold along and we figure to have us a picnic on the way back."

"How'd you do it?" Stocker inquired, eyeing the big Texan with admiration caused by knowing that no other man in the town could claim to be on first name terms with the beautiful blackjack dealer.

"Us Johnny Rebs have to stick by one another in the hostile North," Mark claimed. "And now, sir, you-all's making me keep the lady waiting."

"I wouldn't do that for the world," Stocker asserted and ambled away whistling.

A grin flickered across Mark's lips as he recognized the peace officer's tune was "Dixie." Entering the barn, he decided the slow-moving and sleepy-seeming marshal had far quicker wits than one would think by merely looking at him. He also guessed at the aspect of the shooting which was puzzling Stocker as he too found it curious.

Why would a man holding a shotgun take the time to draw and use a revolver?

Returning to the Bella Union Hotel, Mark Counter found Marigold Tremayne waiting for him. She was dressed in a less elegant, but more functional fashion than on their first meeting. Bare headed, she wore a plain white blouse and black skirt which still showed off her magnificent figure. A picnic basket covered with a clean white cloth was at her feet. In her right hand was a black reticule the same size as the other she had had in the saloon. However, it was the object in her left hand which drew most of his attention.

"I thought you might like to have this along," the blonde remarked, tossing the Texan's Winchester to him. "Don't look so surprised. I told the desk clerk you'd forgotten it and he let me have your key so I could go up and collect it. The wardrobe seemed the most likely place for you to have put it and, sure enough, that's where I found it."

"Only I've got the key in my pocket," Mark pointed out, putting the rifle on the seat and swinging to the ground to collect the basket.

"I didn't really need to ask for the door key either," Marigold answered. "Shall I take the reins?"

"Why sure," Mark assented, refraining from inquiring from where the blonde had acquired her knowledge of picking locks.

There was nothing out of the ordinary in the suggestion, or its acceptance. It had long been a tradition in the West for the woman to drive, leaving the man unimpeded to defend them in an emergency.

Placing the basket on the floor between the front and back seats, Mark helped Marigold aboard and joined her. Showing herself competent to control the spirited horse, she set it moving in accordance with the directions she had received from Pop Larkin when hiring the surrey.

Once clear of the town, the blond giant asked why the girl thought the four hardcases had waylaid her in the alley. She suggested the same reason which he had given to Stocker. In response to his next question, she explained that she had not raised the alarm because the men had threatened to disfigure her if she attempted to do so. His mentioning Wicker's death at the hands of Jubal Framant produced a shudder and a request for a change of subject.

After talking about Elkhorn and comparing it with other towns in a way which suggested she had travelled extensively, Marigold questioned Mark about his association with Calamity Jane. He noticed that she seemed relieved and pleased when he stated he had no permanent, or serious, romantic inclinations in that direction. However, remembering various comments passed by the red head as they were travelling together, he grew even more convinced that he should try to prevent her and the blonde from meeting.

The journey to the ranch house went by pleasantly and without incident. Nor was the time Marigold and Mark stayed there any less enjoyable. If Tom Gamble was disappointed that Dusty Fog had not come in person, he concealed it. Showing no objection to having the well known lady blackjack dealer of the Crystal Palace Saloon in her home, his wife proved a charming and friendly hostess. She insisted that the visitors stayed for lunch and, after an excellent meal, kept the blonde company while her husband conducted his business with the blond giant.

"We won't be needing the picnic basket after all," Mark commented, as he and his beautiful companion were riding away from the ranch house in the surrey.

"I didn't expect we would," Marigold replied. "So all I brought was a bottle of champagne—and two towels."

"*Towels*?" Mark queried. "Why would we need *towels*?"

"Why to *dry* ourselves, of course," Marigold explained, her face taking on an expression of guileless innocence. "Even though we can't chill it properly, we'll just have to wait for the champagne to cool before we drink it. So I thought it might be pleasant if, while we're waiting, we took a swim in that stream we crossed on the way here."

"I thought you said you'd not been out this way before?" the big Texan challenged, but with curiosity rather than any suggestion of suspicion.

"I haven't," the blonde confirmed, showing no annoyance at the question. "That's why I asked the desk clerk if he knew of a place where we could have our picnic on the way back and he suggested the stream. Then I realized that the Gambles would invite us to eat with them. So, as we wouldn't want another meal, I decided just to bring the champagne and the towels."

"You know something, Marigold Tremayne?" the blond giant said admiringly, putting the Winchester on the outside so he could move closer to the blonde. "You're a right smart lil gal."

"I've *never* had the slightest doubts on the matter," Marigold replied, nestling against Mark as he placed an arm around her shoulder and smiling up at him. Then she went on disarmingly, "And I just bet that *Calamity Jane* wouldn't have thought of bringing along either champagne, or towels."

"There's only one thing wrong with your notion," the blond giant pointed out, thinking life was likely to be a whole heap more peaceful if the red head did not return to Elkhorn until after he had headed back to Kansas. His every instinct warned him that she and the blonde were not going to get along if he was around. "I don't have a swimming costume with me."

"Neither do I," Marigold confessed, looking as if butter would have difficulty melting in her mouth. "But I promise I won't peek at you, if you-all don't peek at me."

"You have got a bargain, ma'am," Mark promised, with what appeared to be great solemnity. "Cross my heart and hope to vote Republican should I peek."

"Why I just couldn't ask for anything more reassuring than *that*," the blonde declared. "Nor need to. After all, you behaved in a most gentlemanly manner last night. So I'm certain sure I can count on you-all doing just the same today."

"Why sure," the blond giant answered. "You can count on me to behave just like I did last night."

"That's *exactly* what I am counting on!" Marigold purred.

Guiding the surrey around the bend which brought into view about a hundred yards ahead the wooden bridge built by Gamble across the stream which formed the boundary to his ranch, the blonde's thoughts on the pleasures soon to come were disrupted. The appearance of the vehicle disturbed a small flock of prairie chickens foraging by the side of the trail. Taking flight, the birds made for the bushes on the bank of the stream. However, instead of descending into the shelter of the foliage, they changed direction hurriedly at the last moment.

The sight of the prairie chickens turning aside in such obvious alarm provoked immediate, if involuntary, responses from Marigold and Mark!

Although the blond giant had also been contemplating the pleasures which would shortly be forthcoming, his instincts took control of their own volition. Even as Marigold was bringing the surrey to a halt, he snatched up his Winchester and bounded from it. He did not know what had caused the birds to behave in such a fashion, but was too experienced to take chances. They might merely have been frightened by some kind of animal, but the area would be ideal for anybody who wanted to lay an ambush or waylay travellers along the trail. With such a contingency in mind, on alighting, he worked the lever to charge the rifle's chamber and made a rolling dive which took him to the shelter of a fair sized rock at the side of the trail. Lying prone behind it, he scanned the bushes along the barrel and with his right forefinger ready to squeeze the trigger if necessary.

From all appearances, Marigold was not unused to facing danger. There was no suggestion of panic in her behaviour, only an awareness of what kind of action was called for and what would best serve their purpose if somebody with hostile intentions had frightened off the prairie chickens. Darting forward, she grasped the horse by its headstall. Leading it around, she kept it between her and the bushes until it was facing in the direction from which they had come. When she accomplished this without being shot at, or anything else happening, she stood in front of the animal and continued to use it as a shield.

"Hey, Mark Counter!" called a harsh masculine voice, from amongst the foliage at the point towards which the bird had been making before veering away. "We've no quarrel with *you* over last night. It's *her's* we're after!"

"You won't get her now any more than you did then!" the blond giant answered, deducing that the speaker was one of the men with whom Marigold and he had fought the night before. "She's with me and under *my* protection."

"Then she can't have told you who she is!" the man in the bushes claimed. "She's *Belle Starr*!"

"I know she is!"[1] Mark lied, having glanced at the beautiful blonde and seen the look of distress mingled with contrition on her face as she nodded in silent confirmation. "She told me last night, but that doesn't change a goddamned thing. The only way you-all can get to her is by passing *me*. Which, happen that's the way you want it, come ahead and *try*. I might not be the Ysabel Kid, but I reckon me and this old rifle can do something about stopping you-all."

Being a shrewd psychologist, even though he had never heard the word, the blond giant felt sure the name he had spoken was likely to produce a salutary effect upon the men in the bushes. So did the girl. The Ysabel Kid was well known for his loyalty to his friends and equally famous for the deadly efficient way in which he dealt with enemies. Since Mark had become a member of the OD Connected's floating outfit, he and the Kid had spent much of their time together and in the company of Dusty Fog. She had expected them to be in Elk-

---

1. *We realize this version of how Mark Counter became acquainted with the true identity of "Marigold Tremayne" differs from the events recorded in:* Part One, "The Bounty On Belle Starr's Scalp," TROUBLED RANGE. *However, Mark's grandson, Andrew Mark "Big Andy" Counter assures us that the incident took place as we are now describing. We can only assume that our previous source of information was produced to give Mark credit for possessing greater perception than was the case.* J.T.E.

horn, if not at the saloon, when she had been informed of his identity the previous night and she believed that the speaker and his companions might be under the same impression. If so, assuming that such competent and effective retribution might be close at hand, they might be disinclined to take the chance of bringing it upon themselves.

"I told you we've no quarrel with you," the speaker reminded, with a timbre to his voice which suggested that Mark's reference to his *amigo* had produced the required result. "If she'll cut us in on the booty from the bank in Wichita, we'll back off and leave you be."

"You damned fools!" 'Marigold Tremayne,' shouted, taking her gaze from the big Texan. "I didn't have anything to do with it."

"Toby Wicker told us you did!" the man in the bushes asserted.

"I've never heard of him!" Belle Starr protested.

"He recognized you from back in the Indian Nations," the man claimed. "Which's how we knowed you."

"If he was so slick, how come Framant took him?" Mark challenged. "Belle's telling you the truth. She wasn't in the hold up at Wichita and, even if she had been, do you-all reckon she'd be toting the money around with her?"

"Where'd she chance leaving it?" the man countered.

"She could have left it in the bank at Elkhorn, seeing that nobody's recognized her from the description on the reward dodgers," the blond giant replied. "But she wasn't in the hold up and *doesn't* have it. Now I'm getting quick sick of talking to you-all. So I'm going to count to ten and, happen you've not lit a shuck afore I get there, I'm going to start throwing lead. Which same'll bring some of Tom Gamble's cowhands on the run to find out why. One! Two!"

"Hold it!" yelled a voice from the bushes at the other side of the trail, as the count reached 'seven' and following a brief discussion carried out across it in tones which did not reach Belle and Mark. "We can't pull out. Our hosses are on the other side of the bridge."

"Then go and use them!" Mark authorized and, as a sign of his good faith, leaned his rifle against the side of the rock so the trio could see he was no longer holding it. "I'm not a god-damned bounty hunter like Framant and I won't stop you-all."

"All right!" the first speaker assented urgently. "We're pulling out!"

"Go to it," Mark confirmed. "Only keep to the trail where we can watch you go!"

Behaving more like scared schoolboys detected in mischief than the intended captors of the famous lady outlaw, the three men emerged from their place of ambush. While each held a shoulder arm, only the second speaker had a repeater. This was an old Spencer carbine with an inferior range and rate of fire to the blond giant's Winchester rifle. Backing warily across the bridge, they turned into the bushes at the far side of the stream. Reappearing on their horses after a few seconds, they rode away along the trail as they had been instructed.

"Oh Mark, I'm so *sorry!*" Belle said, coming forward hesitantly, as the trio were disappearing over the horizon. "I should have told you who I really am last night, then you wouldn't have had any of this trouble."

"Maybe not," the blond giant answered gently, taking the girl in his arms. "But only because I might have watched our back trail on the way out. After last night, I'd still have asked you-all to come with me."

"Thank you, Mark, thank you!" Belle breathed, returning the Texan's hug and raising her face to be kissed. "I've *never* had anything said to me I'd rather hear than that."

"You know what riles me, though?" Mark inquired, after their lips parted, still pressing the blonde to him. "Thinking about all that champagne going to waste."

"It doesn't seem fair on the towels not to use them either, after disturbing the poor lil things," Belle went on innocently. "I'm sure those three yacks won't dare come back, so there's no reason we *shouldn't* use them as far as I can see."

"Or me," Mark agreed. "Anyways, I'm game to give it a whirl if you are."

"I *never* could resist a challenge," the lady outlaw claimed. "Let's go and find us a swimming hole, but no *peeking* after we're undressed, mind."

"*Peeking's* the *last* thing on my mind," the blond giant asserted reassuringly.

CHAPTER FOURTEEN

The Toughest Gal in the West

Hearing the soft pad of hurrying feet approaching across his room as he was unlocking and opening the door, Mark Counter was jolted from his state of pleasant reverie just as swiftly as he had been earlier in the day when alerted to the possibility of the ambush by the behaviour of the prairie chickens.

Swimming in the nude like two children, making love and consuming the champagne had taken place without interruption. Nor had there been any reference to the discovery made by the blond giant regarding the true identity of "Marigold Tremayne." Instead, he and the beautiful blonde had given themselves unrestrainedly and without the slightest reservation to each other. It was, although neither realized, the beginning of a relationship which would continue intermittently, growing ever warmer until Belle Starr's death brought it to an end.[1]

While completing the return journey as the sun was going down, without having seen anything further of her would-be captors, the lady outlaw had insisted upon proving to Mark that his faith in her innocence where the robbing of the bank at Wichita was concerned was justified. He had stated this was unnecessary, but she had declared it must be done for her own peace of mind.

Although it was not one which she would be willing to present in person to the sheriff of Wichita County, Belle had a perfect alibi. On the day and at the same time that the robbery was taking place, she had been engaged in pulling the successful "diamond-switch" confidence trick against Ernst "*der*

---

1. *See:* Footnotes 15 *and* 16, APPENDIX TWO. *J.T.E.*

Fliescher" Kramer at the Columbus Grand Hotel in Ellsworth. Holding nothing back, with the exception of the names of the people involved, she had described the whole of her activities —including the gun fight in her room and how she had escaped from the town disguised as an old woman—to the blond giant and brought him up to date on her affairs.

Despite having heard of her supposed participation in the bank robbery while she was making her way to the rendezvous at Elkhorn, the lady outlaw had refused to let it deter her from carrying out the purpose of the visit. However, she had had no way of knowing how long she might have to wait before the jewellery was collected. Being unwilling to accept the restrictions which would have been imposed by remaining in the guise of a woman who was well advanced in years, she was also aware that the arrival of a beautiful and unattached young female was certain to arouse curiosity in the town. Accepting this was unavoidable, she had decided to establish herself so prominently it would convey the impression she had nothing to hide.

Having studied the situation on her arrival, Belle had presented herself to the owner of the Crystal Palace Saloon. Her looks, charm and personality had been sufficient to gain her employment as an unusual, but most effective on that account, blackjack dealer. Nor had she been perturbed when the wanted poster had arrived from Wichita and was placed on display with the others near her table. She had considered the "description" it supplied and the fact that she displayed complete indifference to it had helped to divert any suspicions regarding her true identity.

Despite having handed over the jewels two days earlier, Belle was intending to remain in Elkhorn until another matter had been completed. Wanting to establish her innocence of the bank robbery, she had sent a letter to a lawyer of dubious morals who at that time had his office in Kansas City. It contained sufficient details, such as the contents of the note she had written to Kramer, and the details of the crushed "diamond" on the floor of the room in which she had left what she believed to have been two dead men, to prove she had been in Ellsworth and not Wichita on the day of the hold up. She did not like Counsellor Milton Grosvenor as a person,[2] but had no doubt he was sufficiently competent to ensure the facts were made public thus compelling the sheriff to withdraw the wanted posters.

The lady outlaw had admitted that she had misgivings over the arrival of Jubal Framant in Elkhorn. However, she was counting upon the fact that she had changed the colour of her hair from brunette to blonde and had reached the town by a circuitous route. In addition there was the story of her "previous life" which she had caused to be circulated,[3] and which she hoped would keep her safe from his attentions. When the blond giant had suggested that he should have a confrontation with the bounty hunter, she had made him promise he would not do so. As she had pointed out, she was sure he could survive such an encounter; but, even if he only forced Framant to leave town, he would put her position in jeopardy. Like himself, she had a high opinion of Marshal Joel Stocker's intelligence and believed the event might arouse speculations with regards to her which she would prefer to remain unconsidered.

Beyond requesting and receiving the assurance where the bounty hunter was concerned, neither Belle's nor Mark's plans for the future had been discussed. Nor, for all the warmth of their feelings for one another at that moment, did either consider anything permanent would come of their meeting. Fate had brought them together, but their divergent ways of life precluded any hope at that time of their acquaintance becoming extended by more than a couple of days at the most. Their love-making had been satisfying, most enjoyable and something neither would soon forget, but they mutually and without the need to comment regarded it as no more than a delightful interlude in their respectively eventful lives. Certainly one contingency would not arise from it. Like Calamity Jane, when the matter had been raised by the blond giant, the

2. At a later period of his career, Mark Counter would come into contact with Counsellor Milton Grosvenor. The events in which they participated are recorded in: Part Two, "A Wife For Dusty Fog," THE SMALL TEXAN. J.T.E.

3. The story was that "Marigold Tremayne's" parents had lost their plantation in Louisiana to unscrupulous "Yankee" carpetbaggers and she was trying to raise sufficient money to set them up in business again elsewhere. J.T.E.

blonde was aware of and intended to carry out the Indian method of ensuring no child would result from their association.

Everything Mark had been told and deduced had confirmed his belief that Belle Starr was the most remarkable young woman he had ever met, even including Calamity Jane. He had been impressed by her loyalty and sense of honour in carrying out the delivery of the stolen jewels, even though the man who had hired her was dead. There had been nothing contrite, nor boastful, in the way she had spoken of her criminal activities. She had neither tried to justify, nor excuse, the way in which she lived.

The suggestion that somebody was in his room brought Mark's thoughts about the lady outlaw to an instant stop. It also provoked an instinctive, but very effective, reaction.

Without any need for conscious thought to guide it, the big Texan's right hand dipped to bring out the offside Army Colt. At the same time, his left turned the handle and shoved the door hard. Swinging inwards, it struck something which gave a gasp. Receiving confirmation that he had been correct in his assumption and also gaining an indication of the intruder's position, he lunged into the room. Thrusting the door closed, he turned and lined his revolver. Its hammer was drawn back by his thumb and his forefinger had depressed the trigger.

The barrel lined on the chest of Calamity Jane!

It was the narrowest escape of the happy-go-lucky red head's young life!

If Calamity had been dealing with a less competent handler of firearms, she would have been killed!

As it was, such was the quickness of the blond giant's wits and so superbly attuned his reflexes that he was *just* able to refrain from releasing the Colt's hammer!

Having retreated a couple of steps when the door flew open and hit her, the girl was standing like a statue. Although she was frightened by the realization that she was covered by a cocked and loaded weapon, its trigger depressed and only the thumb preventing the hammer from falling, it did not show on her pretty, freckled face.

'My, aren't *you* the jumpy one today?" Calamity asked, but there was a slight tremour in her voice which indicated her appreciation of how close she had been to death.

"God damn you, Calam!" Mark fumed, after the moment he required to bring his churning emotions sufficiently under control so he was able to lower the Colt's hammer safely instead of allowing it to be propelled on to the waiting percussion cap under the impulsion of the mechanism. "You surely like to live dangerously!"

"Dangerously my ass!" the red head replied, in a voice which still throbbed with nervous tension. "I only aimed to give you a lil surprise!"

Then, as the blond giant returned the Colt to its holster, the girl ran forward to throw herself into his arms. Her hands went around him and, crushing close, he could feel her heart pounding against him. After a moment, she raised her face and her mouth reached hungrily to his. Following the long, hard, almost brutal kiss, which allowed them both to regain their respective composure, she moved clear and, cocking her head on one side, studied him for a few seconds.

"Whee-dogie!" Calamity ejaculated at the end of the scrutiny, in her normal tone. "I sure put my brand on you. Smack under the right—Hey! That son-of-a-bitch isn't *mine*! Mark Counter what have you been up to while I've been gone?"

"Would you-all believe I cut myself *shaving*?" the big Texan inquired, noticing the girl sounded more curious than jealous or antagonistic over the suggestion of his previous night's activities.

"No more'n if you told me you'd got chomped on by a catamount."

"Then what do *you* reckon happened?"

"I just wouldn't want to *guess*."

Deciding that the conversation was approaching an impasse, or rather an area he would rather avoid, Mark concluded he would be advised to let his actions speak instead of words. Scooping the girl up, he kissed her. His action proved only partially successful, he discovered.

"Had I a suspicious mind, I'd say *that* was done to make me quit asking questions," Calamity declared, on being released. Then she went on with a transparent innocence equal to that Belle Starr had employed when suggesting the poker game, "Let's you and me hooraw the town after we've fed. There's a swell looking saloon next door."

"Hell, that's a mite fancy for hoorawing, Calam-gal!"

Mark objected. "There're other places where we'd—!"

"Maybe they don't have blackjack tables," the red head interrupted, her voice filled with a spurious mildness. "Which I'm took with the notion of playing it tonight."

"*Blackjack?*" the blond giant said, raising his eyebrows.

"*Blackjack!*" Calamity confirmed, before Mark could continue with his objection. "They tell me there's a dealer next door who plays near on as well as she totes a picnic basket."

Stepping away from the big Texan as she concluded the comment, the red head put her hands on her hips and grinned. Seeing her even white teeth flashing and her expressive eyes sparkling with merriment, he could not help smiling back. There was something infectious about her zest for living. While she did not conform to the rigid conventions imposed upon most women in that day and age, she clearly enjoyed every moment to the full.

Suddenly Mark remembered how, as he had set her down at the hotel prior to returning the surrey to the livery barn. Belle had looked when suggesting he brought Calamity to the saloon so they could meet. They might, he concluded, have been cast from the same mould. One could not judge either by the same moral standards as other women. Each lived her life the way she felt it should be lived, yet retained a strick code of behaviour from which she would not deviate. The only real difference between them was the way in which fate had guided their careers. While the red head stayed on the right side of the law and engaged in honest, if unconventional for one of her sex, toil, the blonde indulged in criminal activities.

"How'd you-all get to know about Marigold and me?" the blond giant asked wryly.

"Why I didn't reckon's how you'd've rid out with her plain for all to see had you wanted to keep it a secret," Calamity replied. "I heard tell about it soon's I asked where-at you was bedding down."

"Blast Pop Larkin!" Mark snorted, making an accurate guess at the source of the information, although far from annoyed. "I never yet met a livery barn owner who didn't talk the hind leg off a hoss. But how did you-all get in *here*?"

"Told the maid I was your long-lost cousin from Texas."

"And she believed you-all?"

"Either me, or the dollar I gave her to open up," Calamity

asserted, then glanced at the big Texan's neck. "Did *she* give you the other one?"

"The maid?" Mark inquired, deliberately misunderstanding.

"That she-male picnic basket-toting blackjack dealer," the red head clarified patiently.

"She's a Southron lady," the blond giant stated evasively, drawing up his bandana to conceal the two marks.

"Which don't tell me 'yes' nor 'no,'" Calamity grinned. "Go and wash up. Then we'll take us a meal afore we head to the Crystal Palace and play us some blackjack."

Although Mark Counter hoped to delay the meeting between Calamity Jane and Belle Starr until at least the following morning, this was not to be. As he and the red head were entering the passage to go downstairs to the dining-room, he saw the door of the blonde's room open. From what he saw as she emerged, he guessed she had learned of Calamity's arrival and suspected she had been waiting for them to put in an appearance. She was dressed in her working clothes, with the wide brimmed hat and the shawl positioned so it left the decollete of her gown exposed. Carrying the reticule in her left hand, she advanced with a more sensual gait than he had seen until then.

"Why, Mark-honey!" the beautiful blonde greeted, as she converged with the red head and the big Texan at the top of the stairs. "You-all never told me that the *Ysabel Kid* was in town."

While the light in the passage was poor, Mark knew it was not *that* inadequate!

What was more, if the way Calamity moved closer to him was any indication, so did she. He prepared to grab her if she should try to jump Belle, which proved he did not know her very well. Although her first inclination had been to launch a physical attack, she knew this was neither the time nor the place to employ such tactics.

"They do say older women can't see any too good," the red head countered. "Is this that old auntie from Texas you was telling me about, *Mark-honey*?"

"Land-sakes a-mercy!" Belle gasped in well simulated shock, her right hand fluttering to her mouth and eyes running over the other girl from head to toe. "*However* could I have made such a *foolish* mistake when I've always heard the Ysabel Kid is *slim* and good looking."

"That's a real cute dress you're wearing," Calamity purred, subjecting the blonde to a similar scrutiny. "'Course, it'd look better had they one to fit you."

"I was just wondering how much your clothes had cost," Belle replied. "I'm sure you-all bought them for an absurd figure."

"What kind of bottle does that white hair come from?" the red head wanted to know. "It sure hides the grey."

"Perhaps you'd like to see how much *grey* there is in it?" the blonde challenged.

"I was just going to say, 'Why'n't we go somewhere so's I can do just that?'" Calamity claimed, standing tense as a compressed coil spring.

"And I'd be *delighted* to oblige you-all," Belle answered. "But, unfortunately, I have to go to work as soon as Mark and I have had dinner."

"You didn't tell me your old auntie was coming along, Mark," the red head commented, looking at the blond giant accusingly.

"Perhaps you'd better introduce us, Mark-honey," Belle suggested.

"Miss Tremayne, allow me to present Miss Martha Jane Canary," the big Texan obliged with almost solemn formality, despite feeling like a man who was sitting on a keg of gun powder to which a burning fuse was attached. "Miss Canary, this is Miss Marigold Tremayne."

Using the blonde's alias did not imply a lack of trust in the red head. It was merely that Mark considered the secret of Belle's true identity was not his to impart. What was more, remembering certain remarks passed by Calamity when they were discussing the lady outlaw during the journey to Elkhorn, he felt sure the disclosure would remove any chance of avoiding a physical confrontation between the girls. As it was, he believed Belle would be sufficiently aware of her present situation to follow the path of discretion.

"Good heavens, Miss Canary," the blonde remarked, matching the red head's squeeze with one just as powerful as they started to shake hands. Although her expression did not change, her voice gave a suggestion of the struggle in which she was engaged as she continued, "For a moment I thought you-all might be that *Calamity Jane* person one hears about *occasionally.*"

"That could be 'cause I am that *Calamity Jane* person one hears about more than occasional!" the red head responded, gritting out the words with what she hoped to be an air of blatantly false modesty, striving to refrain from displaying her feelings. "But I can't say's how I've ever heard of *you*, not even that often."

"Some of us consider it vulgar to have our names bandied about," Belle asserted, conceding she had met her equal in strength. "Shall we go and eat dinner? I don't care to be late for work."

Despite her comment, Belle Starr did not follow her established procedure of going upstairs to remove her hat and shawl immediately on entering the Crystal Palace Saloon. A number of glances and *sotto voce* remarks were exchanged between the other occupants of the barroom as she accompanied Calamity Jane and Mark Counter to the counter. It was the first time since her arrival in Elkhorn that she had done such a thing. In fact, previously she had invariably politely, but firmly, declined every offer to take a drink.

"What'll it be, ladies?" the blond giant asked, his manner that of one who felt himself being carried along by forces beyond his control.

Having mutually—if silently—decided to declare the trial of strength a stand off, Mark had been amused to notice that each girl had studiously avoided giving any indication of how much pain she had experienced while squeezing rather than shaking hands. Although they were successful facially, both had contrived to work their throbbing fingers in a way which at least partially disguised the real reason. Then, each taking an arm, they had descended the stairs with the big Texan. Despite having continued to exchange far from complimentary remarks all through the meal, they had otherwise been on their best behaviour. Neither had said anything to imply she suspected how close the other had been to him. In fact, for all the interest they showed in him, their respective love-making with him might never have taken place.

"Whiskey for me," Calamity replied.

"I'll have a brandy, *please*, Mark-honey," Belle requested.

"*Brandy!*" the red head snorted. "French hawg-wash!"

"A *lady* doesn't drink whiskey," the blonde countered. "It's *fattening*. Of course, dear, with a figure like yours, what have you-all to lose?"

"Not a thing," Calamity purred back. "At *my* age, you can eat and drink anything you've a mind. It's only you old women's have to go careful."

Once more, in spite of her lack of formal education, the red head had come back with a response which relied upon wit and not profanity. She was, in fact, enjoying the exchanges and did not intend to be considered the loser because she was first to resort to a physical reaction instead of words. Guessing at her feelings on the subject, Mark began to experience a slight sensation of relief.

It did not last for long!

Twisting the glass of whiskey between her fingers, Calamity turned her back to the bar. Resting her elbows on it, she glanced around her while awaiting "Marigold's" next effort. Her gaze halted on the wooden board, paying particular attention to the comment which had been added to the wanted poster from Wichita.

"The toughest gal in the West?" the red head read, each word coming in an explosively derisive snort. "That's not right at all."

Putting down her glass, Calamity went to the board. Digging a stump of pencil from her pocket with her right hand, she rested the left on the table which had been placed beneath it.

"That's *better!*" the red head announced, having written '2nd' between the words, 'The' and 'toughest."

At the counter, the blonde let out a low hiss and clenched her fists.

"Easy, Belle!" Mark warned, grasping her arm. "Calam doesn't know who you are. At least, I haven't told her. And Framant's sat over there."

For a moment, the blond giant thought the lady outlaw would show at least sufficient sense to wait until Calamity rejoined them before taking any action. The hope did not come to fruition.

"Let's just pretty up ole Belle a mite while I'm at it," the red head went on and began to pencil in a moustache on the top lip of the illustration.

Calamity did not notice that Belle had crossed to her side. Watching her, Mark raised and shook his right leg to relieve the pain caused when she delivered a kick which caused him to release her. Then he gave a shrug and leaned on the counter. He was resigned to the fact that, as things were developing, he could not stop the inevitable.

CHAPTER FIFTEEN

How Do *You* Figure in on This?

Silence fell over the barroom of the Crystal Palace Saloon!

With one exception, everybody was staring at "Marigold Tremayne" in something close to amazement!

Dropping her reticule on the table, the beautiful blonde plucked the pencil from its user's fingers. Before the startled Calamity Jane could appreciate exactly what was happening, she had been rammed by Belle Starr's hip and sent staggering a few steps. Having done so, her assailant began to scratch out her amendment to the unofficial information added to the wanted poster.

"I've never met the lady," the blonde claimed, conscious of the puzzlement her far from typical behaviour—where the denizens of the saloon were concerned—was causing and aware that Jubel Framant was studying her speculatively. "But I'm positive the original sentiment was correct!"

Although Belle realized she was behaving in a highly ill-advised fashion, the reckless streak in her nature—about which Sammy Crane had commented to Blue Duck at the railroad depot in Ellsworth, Kansas, after seeing the bounty hunter arrive—refused to yield to the suggestions from the more calculating and sober side of her brain which was advocating a more discreet course. Nor were her feelings where Mark Counter was concerned solely responsible for her actions. Every instinct she possessed assured her that there was nothing between the red head and the blond giant which approached the depth of his emotions over herself. No matter what had taken place between them, Calamity would never be as close to his affections as she knew herself to be. In fact, she sensed that the happy-go-lucky red head appreciated and was

willing to accept the true state of affairs. What stood between
them was something far more elemental than just rivalry over
a desirable man. Recognizing each other as kindred spirits,
neither would be willing to extend to the other the complete
friendship each was hoping for until she was certain it was
deserved by the recipient.

Unbuckling her gunbelt as she returned, Calamity put it on
the table next to the blonde's reticule and, drawing the coiled
bull whip free just as deliberately, she placed it by them. Then
she dipped her right shoulder to deliver a charge which sent
Belle reeling. Managing to keep on her feet, the blonde came
to a halt. However, she was unable to prevent her hat sliding
forward over her eyes. Brushing it off and discarding the
shawl in the same motion, she stood glaring for a moment to
where the red head had picked up the pencil and was turning
to the poster once more.

Hearing Belle approaching Calamity twisted around to face
her. Instead of attempting to avoid what was clearly intended
as an attack, the red head sat on the table and raised her feet
ready to thrust the blonde away. Seeing what was planned,
Belle halted just out of range and reached with both hands.
Although she failed to grasp Calamity by the ankles, she managed to catch hold of the cuffs of the buckskin pants. A yelp
of surprise mingled with anger burst from the red head as the
blonde began to pull and back away.

Despite clutching wildly, Calamity failed to find anything
she could grip and prevent herself from being dragged off the
table. She landed supine on the floor and, to the accompaniment of laughter and shouts of encouragement from the on-
lookers, the blonde continued to haul her across the room.
Nor, for all the thrusting and jerking with her legs, or attempts
to catch hold of something in her hands, was she able to bring
the humiliating progress to a halt.

There was, Calamity realized, only one way out of her
predicament. It was not a means which a more modest and
conventional young woman would have cared to contemplate,
but she did not hesitate. Taking advantage of Belle looking
away, she unbuckled the waist belt and, opening the fly of her
pants, started to wriggle from them. For a few seconds, it
seemed that even this drastic solution was doomed to failure.
Cursing the tight fit of the garments, she managed to grab the

leg of a faro table she was passing. It proved firm enough to restrain her.

Having been looking over her shoulder to make sure she had a clear path to the front door, Belle was unaware of what her captive had done. Finding herself brought to a stop, she returned her gaze to the front and gave a harder tug. Helped by this and a violent wriggling of her hips, Calamity gave a heave which brought her liberty. However, in doing so, she lost her moccasins and left the pants in the blonde's hands. Against that, she gained an unexpected and much needed respite. Taken by surprise, the energy Belle had applied to the pull caused her to stagger backwards until she tripped and, dropping the other girl's discarded garment, sat on her rump.

Coming to her feet, Calamity made an attractive sight. Flapping around her shapely bare legs, the tail of her shirt gave glimpses of the new white, lace-frilled combination chemise and drawers she had bought that afternoon to prove to Mark Counter she was a real lady at heart. They were the latest fashion among female entertainers, short legged and daring and she had the kind of figure to set them off to their best advantage.

Having risen, the red head dived towards the seated blonde. Rolling over on to her shoulders, Belle brought up her bent legs and, as Calamity landed on her feet, straightened them. Employing all the force she could produce via her gluteus, thigh and calf muscles, she propelled the red head backwards. By the time Calamity's involuntary retreat was ended by running into the arms of two men, who saved her from falling and shoved her forward once more, the blonde had risen and was coming to meet her.

Studying the apparently wild and unscientific way in which "Marigold" was advancing, the red head felt somewhat disappointed. She had hoped for something better from the blonde. Having learned how much more effective than hair pulling a clenched fist could be, she felt sure that her knowledge would supply an advantage over the untrained girl as it had in other fights.

"First one into her belly," Calamity thought. "Then the next to her jaw and *then* I'll show her what it feels like to be hauled around by the feet."

The fist drove into the stomach!

Rising, the second set of knuckles met the descending chin!

And Calamity hit the floor on her rump, her head spinning!

The red head had learned a lesson!

"Marigold's" lack of science had been a pose and she knew how to use her fists!

However, having proved that point, Belle showed that Calamity was not alone in being over confident. Hitching her skirt up, she walked forward to draw back her left foot for a kick. Instantly, the red head produced a counter which demonstrated how she had profited from the lessons she had received in other forms of self defence. Hooking her right foot behind the blonde's right ankle and the left on the knee, she pulled on the former and pushed at the latter. Balance destroyed, despite being compelled to topple backwards, Belle's skill as a horsewoman enabled her to break the worst of the fall with her hands.

Coming up almost simultaneously, the girls flung themselves at each other. For a time, it might have been two men fighting. They used their fists, wrestling holds and throws, but few of the tactics usually employed by women. Forming a rough circle about them, but leaving plenty of room for movement, the crowd yelled advice and encouragement. Here and there, gamblers were taking bets on the result. The wagers were being offered at even money, due to there being nothing to give an indication of which girl might win, they were so evenly matched.

"Howdy, Mark," greeted a sleepy voice.

"Howdy, Joel," the blond giant answered, turning his gaze from where Belle and Calamity were slugging it out toe to toe and looking at the speaker. "What are you-all figuring to do about this, speaking as a duly appointed officer of the law?"

"Ain't doing nothing yet a-whiles," the town marshal answered, nodding to where the girls had gone into a wrestling clinch. "My job's to keep the peace, which starting a riot 'cause I was to horn in and spoil them ladies settling their differences private-like wouldn't be doing. How do you figure in on this?"

"You could say it was me who brought them together," Mark admitted. "But, knowing Calamity, she'd've come in here and tangled with somebody and, after hearing about us,

B—'Marigold' would be the most likely for her to pick on."

"Huh huh!" Stocker grunted. "I sort of saw it that way my own self. Which it's lucky for Miss Marigold, her being such a for real lady, she knows how to hold up her end in a fight."

At that moment, her prevously elegant gown torn down the side and showing underclothing as scanty for the period as that worn by her opponent, the "for real lady" was swinging Calamity around by the hair. Being released, the red head ran helplessly backwards to crash against the wall. Although she did not go down, she stood on spread apart feet and was clearly dazed by the impact.

"Looks like it's over," the marshal commented, watching the dishevelled blonde following Calamity. "We'd best st—!"

The comment went unfinished as Belle halted before the red head. Instead of delivering the kick to which the other was exposed, she started to swing her hands. Not in punches which would have rendered the recipient hors-de-combat, but in slaps to the face which jolted her head side to side. Pain jolted Calamity from the dazed condition, but her response was instinctive. Thrusting herself from the wall, she sent her hands into the no longer immaculate blonde hair and the squeal this elicited proved she had recovered sufficiently for the pulling to hurt.

Reacting just as instinctively, Belle also grabbed hair and the fight turned to more feminine methods. Reeling across the room, the girls seemed to be enveloped in a flailing tangle of arms and legs which jerked at hair, swung punches or slaps, or kicked wildly. For several minutes, they gave an excellent display of distaff barroom brawling whether on their feet or rolling over and over across the floor.

Gaining the upper position, her shirt ripped down the front and minus its left sleeve, Calamity grabbed for a double handful of blonde hair with the intention of using it and banging Belle's head on the floor. Realizing what was planned, Belle curled her feet forward between the red head's arms and sides as if performing a full nelson with her legs. Giving a yell as she was hauled backwards, Calamity continued to roll. Alighting on her feet, she once again essayed a dive and was met by Belle's raised feet. Hurtled backwards, she landed on the top of a table. As Belle advanced, she came off it and ducked her head. Going in, bent at the waist, she butted the blonde full in the bosom. With her advance turned into an agonized retreat, Belle caused the crowd to scatter and blundered with some force against the bar. Only by clinging to it was she able to keep her feet and, at that moment, she was as unable to protect herself as Calamity had been when thrown into the wall.

"We'd best stop Calam," Mark suggested, as the red head came across the room.

"It'd be best," Stocker assented, sharing the blond giant's belief that the girl might be too enraged to extend the kind of leniency she had received.

Once again, however, the need for the men to intercede did not arise!

"H—Had enough?" Calamity asked, halting just out of reaching distance.

"N—No!" Belle replied, bracing herself for the attack she expected.

It did not come!

"H—Hold it!" the red head requested, making no attempt to raise her hands.

"H—Have—y—*you*—had—enough?"   the   blonde croaked just as breathlessly and in surprise.

"L—Like—hell—!" Calamity declared, stepping forward until she too was leaning against the counter. "F—Feel like— a—drink afore we come to taw again, happen that's all right with you."

"I—It is," Belle confirmed, turning. "F—Fred, whiskey and brandy!"

The low rumble of discontent which had arisen died away as the spectators began to appreciate what was happening. Everybody had expected Calamity to finish off "Marigold" and even those who were betting on the well-liked blackjack dealer were feeling cheated by the suggestion of such an indecisive ending. Now they realized that the combatants were merely taking a breathing spell and liquid refreshments to help revive them before resuming hostilities.

"My call," Calamity announced, having tossed down the whiskey in a grateful gulp and paying no attention to Mark who was standing close by. "Same again, Fred."

"Here's looking at you-all, Calam," Belle toasted, also ignoring the blond giant and raising the glass which the bartender had replenished once again without requesting payment. "Not that *you'll* be seeing much out of your left eye comes morning."

"If it looks worse than that mouse I've put under your right, it's bad for sure," the red head asserted, studying the blonde's bruised cheek judiciously. "Hey, 'Marigold' gal, where did *you* learn to fight this good?"

"It seemed a sensible thing to do," Belle replied, returning her glass to the counter as Calamity was doing. "Are you ready?"

"Sure," the red head confirmed and lashed around a backhand blow.

Caught on the jaw an instant before she could strike, Belle rocked back a couple of steps. However, she retaliated with a punch as Calamity turned and the fight was resumed with close to its original vigour. Nor, so close were they in size, weight and skill, was there any sign of either gaining more than a brief domination of the action. Once the blonde seemed to be getting the upper hand, having the red head on the floor and trapped in what wrestlers called a stepover toehold, but a kick in the bosom from the free foot caused her to release the captured leg. Not long after, Calamity gained a stranglehold from behind and lost it when Belle's struggles permitted her to slam her elbows backwards in a painful manner.

Gradually and inevitably, the pace and energy being expended by the embattled pair began to take its toll. In fact, it was a tribute to their superb physical condition, courage and determination that they lasted so long. Each missed opportunities as the minutes dragged by to land a *coup de grace* upon the other. No longer did their slaps land with whip-like cracks, arriving instead as something closer to pushes than blows. Little of their earlier skill was in evidence either, having been replaced by almost mindless mauling, pushing and clutching.

There was no longer any trace of the cool, calm and elegant "Marigold Tremayne" which had endeared Belle to almost everybody she had met in Elkhorn. Her erstwhile immaculate hair now resembled a tangled, dirty, blonde woollen mop. Sweat and dirt streaked her distorted face, its right eye swollen almost shut and nose bloody. At some time in the conflict, her left hand had been bitten and she would carry the scar to her grave. Her gown and shoes were long since gone, her black stockings hung in tatters and her undergarments had not escaped unscathed. Calamity was just as badly bruised, battered and soaked in perspiration, in addition to her attire having suffered equally.

"I don't take kind to having to spoil their fun," Stocker remarked, after close to fifteen minutes unremitting conflict had caused so much destruction to the girls' clothing that both were stripped to the waist. "But it wouldn't be right to let them lose what's left."

"I'm with you on *that*," Mark answered without hesitation. "And I'll back your play any which way you-all aim to take it."

Even as the decision was being reached, it was rendered unnecessary.

Tottering on legs which looked as soft and yielding as heat buckled candles, the girls came together in a clinch. As they struggled weakly, hooking a foot behind Calamity's ankle by accident rather than any conscious intention, Belle caused them both to lose their balance. Still locked in each others arms, they stumbled and their heads hit the wall. The impact was only glancing, but sufficient in their enfeebled and exhausted state. Crumpling like two rag dolls from which the stuffing had been removed, they went down and rolled apart. Each lay on her back, arms thrown out and bosoms heaving, but with no other movement on either's part.

"What'd you-all call *that, amigo*?" the blond giant inquired, as silence fell over the crowd. "Speaking as a duly appointed officer of the law, that is."

"I'd say's a stand off'd be about right," the marshal answered. "Now I reckon we'd best see to them, don't you?"

"Why sure," Mark assented. "If you'll fetch the doctor to the hotel so's he can look them over, I'll have them carried there."

"Count on a blasted Johnny Reb to pick himself the best chore," Stocker stated, although he was aware that his superior knowledge of the town made him the more suitable to summon medical assistance, his words almost being drowned by the cheers which followed the floor manager's announcement of drinks on the house to toast the two gallant fighters. "Let's get to it."

•   •   •   •

After pocketing the skeleton key with which he had unfastened the lock, Dexter Soskin looked furtively along the upstairs passage of the Bella Union Hotel. Satisfied that he was unobserved, which was hardly surprising as the time was almost two o'clock in the morning, he started to open the door of the room wherein an examination of the register at the reception desk earlier had suggested he would find the person for whom he had come to search in Elkhorn. Despite the condition in which she had been when he last saw her, he drew and cocked his Colt 1860 Army revolver before entering. He was hoping she would be sufficiently recovered to answer his question and, remembering what had taken place during their previous meeting, he was disinclined to take chances.

On discovering that "Cornelia von Blücherdorf" had succeeded in giving him the slip at Ellsworth, Kansas, Soskin had started to follow the false trail left by her two part-Cherokee assistants and Joy Turner. A chance remark about the girl's facial injuries, which were seen by a maid at a hotel in St. Louis, Missouri, one morning before she covered them with make-up, had warned him of his error far sooner than might otherwise have been the case. Still determined to gain possession of the jewels, he had started back westwards and picked up a clue to the whereabouts of the "brunette" in Kansas City. Although he had only recently returned to the West after spending a couple of years in and around New York City, where he had posed as a wealthy rancher, he had kept in touch with various criminal associates in Kansas. One of them had supplied sufficient information for him to have considered it warranted investigation.

Reaching Elkhorn earlier in the night, Soskin had taken a room at the Bella Union Hotel. He had, in fact, arrived shortly after the woman he was seeking left the premises. Suspecting she had changed her appearance prior to leaving Ellsworth, he had not been discouraged when his inquiries established there was nobody answering to "Cornelia's" description in Elkhorn. Hearing a reference to the beautiful blonde blackjack dealer at the Crystal Palace Saloon, he had arrived there during the later stages of the fight. Despite her far from elegant appearance, he had recognized her. Returning to the hotel, he had learned which room she was occupying and, retiring to his own quarters, had waited until what he considered to be a suitable hour to pay her a visit. His gentle knock had elicited no response and he had had no difficulty in gaining admittance.

Peering cautiously into the room and ready to make a hurried withdrawal should the need arise, Soskin saw no cause for alarm. The lamp on the sidepiece was lit, but its wick had been turned down. This caused the large wardrobe at the right side and the other fittings to be in the shadows. He could, however, see a shape completely covered by the covers of the bed. It made no movement to suggest his presence had been detected as he silently advanced, and its stillness made him wonder if the battered blonde had been so heavily sedated by the doctor, who had arrived with the town marshal, that she was unconscious instead of merely sleeping.

Hoping such was not the case, Soskin reached with his left hand to draw back the covers. Instantly, he knew something was radically wrong. Neither blonde hair nor bruised features met his gaze. Instead, he stared down at a pillow laid lengthwise where the woman's head should have been.

Even as the realization struck Soskin, he heard a creaking from the wardrobe. Turning his head, he saw its door flying open and a big masculine shape lunged out. Alarmed by the discovery that he was not alone, he swung his Colt hurriedly in the direction of the danger and squeezed its trigger.

Concerned by the possibility that Jubal Framant suspected the true identity of 'Marigold Tremayne' and meant to try and collect the bounty offered on her, Mark Counter had decided to take precautions. After the doctor had attended to the injuries sustained by Belle Starr and Calamity Jane, he had waited until the passage was deserted. Going to the blonde's room and using the pass key which had been given to him so he could keep his eye on them, he had taken her to his quarters. Then, determined to end the threat posed by the bounty hunter, he had made the preparations which deceived the intruder. On hearing the knock, he had concealed himself in the wardrobe ready to deal with whoever came in.

Although surprised to find the intruder was not Framant, the response provoked by his appearance left Mark in no doubt as to what he must do. Nor was he deterred by the bullet which whistled by close to his head. He too held an Army Colt ready for use in his right hand and he was far more skilled than his assailant. Cutting loose two shots so rapidly the sounds could not be discerned separately, he drove the bullets into the centre of the man's chest.

Thrown backwards with the revolver dropping from his hand, Soskin was far less fortunate than he had been in the room at the Columbus Grand Hotel. Then he was only wounded and stunned. On this occasion, he was dead before he sprawled supine on the floor.

"Well," Mark said quietly, crossing to turn the lamp's light higher. "I don't know who *you* are, *hombre*, but it could be you've saved that bastard Framant's life."

CHAPTER SIXTEEN

That's Not Why *You* Want Her

"Good morning, Miss Calamity, Mark," Marshal Joel Stocker greeted, strolling up as the blond giant was helping the red-head—who was clearly feeling stiff and sore—on to the box of her wagon. Glancing to where the bloodbay stallion was standing saddled and with its reins fastened to the tailgate, he went on, "I wouldn't've reckoned you'd feel up to pulling out this morning."

"I've work waiting for me," Calamity Jane replied, sitting down with a wince and managing to put on a wry grin. "Anyways, I reckoned you'd be happy to see us go. Say, happen you see good ole "Marigold," say goodbye for me and tell her I'm sorry I had to hand her such a licking last night."

"I'll say you handed her a *licking*," the peace officer responded, studying the red head's battered features. "She never laid a hand on you."

"Then why didn't you stop the crowd doing it?" Calamity demanded in mock indignation. "Because, happen *she* didn't, *somebody* was sure pounding hell out of me. You'll pass my word to her, though, won't you?"

"I'd admire to," Stocker asserted sleepily. "Only she's gone."

"Gone?" Calamity gasped. "What do you mean, she's gone?"

"She wasn't at the Bella Union when I went around to have words with her just now," the marshal explained. "Seems she took all her gear, left enough money to pay for the room and lit a shuck out of there."

"What'd you want the words about?" the red head inquired.

"Was wondering happen she might know that feller's Mark had to shoot in her room last night, among other things," Stocker explained. "Or didn't you know about *that*?"

"Sure I knowed about it," Calamity claimed. "Mark told me while we was eating breakfast. Allowed it was just some son-of-a-bitch figuring to rob her."

"Yeah, that's what he told me," Stocker conceded, nothing in his tone indicating whether he accepted or disbelieved the explanation. "Got much of a load on, Calam?"

"Not a whole heap," the red head answered. "Just me and Mark's gear."

Walking to the rear of the wagon in an apparently lethargic fashion, the peace officer looked beneath the open canopy. Apart from a couple of wooden boxes, two bed rolls and something oblong in shape covered by a buffalo robe, the interior was bare. Passing around and behind the bloodbay, he strolled forward in the same unhurried manner. While doing so, he stepped over a pile of dried buffalo chips and a few logs which lay between the side of the vehicle and the corral in which its team had been left overnight.

"What's up, Joel?" the red head challenged, but without anger. "Did you reckon's she could've snuck in the back and hid without me knowing?"

"Nope," Stocker admitted. "Not without you *knowing*."

"Have you-all seen anything of Framant, Joel?" Mark inquired, watching the peace officer and deciding, as no suggestion of his true thoughts could be discerned from his expression or voice, he would make a very dangerous opponent in a game of poker.

"Sure," Stocker confirmed. "He allows's how 'Miss Marigold's' wrong about thinking she's seen him trailing her from place to place. Reckons he's never seen her afore he got here."

"Looks like I lost a night's sleep for nothing, then," the blond giant drawled, wondering how much of his explanation for having been in 'Marigold Tremayne's' room to deal with the intruder was accepted by the bland-featured marshal.

"Not all the way for nothing," Stocker corrected. "You stopped that jasper robbing her. Well, I reckon I'll go and grab me a bite to eat. See you both again sometime, maybe?"

"Let's hope so," Mark agreed, going to unfasten and mount

his bloodbay. "Only the next time, we'll try to keep things more peaceable."

A sleepy grin played upon the marshal's face as he watched the blond giant riding eastwards alongside the wagon. Then, turning on his heel, he walked away. In passing, he gave one of the dried buffalo chips a deliberate kick and his grin grew even broader.

Waiting until the peace officer was out of sight, Jubal Framant came from where he had been watching Calamity and Mark completing the preparations for their departure. He was accompanied by a couple of surly faced, poorly shaven men whose attire and the bull whips on their belts implied they were in similar employment to the red head. Stocker would have recognized them as Hobie Carver and Fred Varney. Along with a third associate, they operated two freight wagons which came and went on occasion with loads of an unspecified nature to be delivered to destinations they never discussed.

"Well she *wasn't* hid in the wagon," Carver stated. "And I never figured she would be, comes to that. Not after the way she fought with Calam last night."

"Counter could have talked that red head bitch into doing it," Framant pointed out, scowling at the speaker. Needing the trio's assistance if his suspicions should prove correct, he restrained his annoyance and went on, "Wherever she went after she left the hotel, it couldn't have been far. You saw the red head. She looked like she could hardly walk and Starr wouldn't be in any better shape."

"Is she *Bell Star*?" Varney asked. "She doesn't look nothing like how it says she looks on that wanted poster from Wichita."

"It *is* her!" Framant declared with assurance. "Wicker told me he recognized her just afore I shot him."

"What'd she do to old Lard-Gut Jeb to make him set *you* on her trail?" Carver inquired, wondering how the outlaw had had time to supply the information when—according to the story repeated to Stocker in their presence that morning—he had begun to draw his gun as soon as he was confronted by the bounty hunter, but deciding it would be inadvisable to raise the point.

"If you're so god-damned interested in *his* business, why

don't you ask *him* the next time you meet up?" Framant suggested, in a tone which indicated he considered that aspect of the matter was closed. Without correcting the misapprehension regarding the identity of the man by whom he was hired, he went on, "All I know is I've been paid to get her and was told I could call on any of his men should I reckon I needed help. Or don't *you* aim to give it now I've asked?"

"We'll help you!" Varney promised hurriedly, having such a bad reputation he would have difficulty in persuading any other freight outfit to hire him. "All *you* have to do is take us to her and tell us what you want doing."

"I'm not going up against Joel Stocker happen she's still in his bailiwick!" Carver asserted in a determined fashion, despite being equally dependant upon remaining in his present employment. "And, the way Calam looked, I can't see how she could've left unless she was helped."

"You can bet your god-damned life she's been *helped*!" Framant declared, looking at the buffalo chips and logs which had attracted the marshal's attention. "Come, we'll pick up Lensinger and get after her."

"Anybody coming after us, Mark?" Calamity Jane inquired, after she and the blond giant had put some three miles between themselves and Elkhorn, feeling too stiff and sore to try to look to the rear.

"Nope," Mark Counter replied, having been keeping watch on the trail behind them. "Who're you-all expecting, Joel Stocker?"

"Nope," the red head answered. "He's *town* marshal and we're way clear of his bailiwick. Anyways, he wouldn't figure it was worth following us. We sure put one over on him, way we pulled out."

"Reckon we did, huh?"

"Don't you?"

"I'd sooner say 'no' than 'yes' to *that*."

"You mean he—?" Calamity began, swinging around more quickly than she intended so that the pain brought her words to a halt.

"If he *didn't*, I'll kiss Wyatt Earp's butt," Mark declared, feeling sure that Stocker was aware of their reason for leaving town.

"I'll drop by and thank him next time I'm out this way," Calamity declared. Then, grinning and accepting the discomfort she experienced as she leaned over the side of the box, she continued speaking in a much louder voice than the situation appeared to warrant. "Hey, Mark. I reckon I'll go straight on through that ford ahead and water my team on the other side. The bottom of the wagon needs washing."

"You just *do*, red top!" Belle Starr's voice yelled from beneath the vehicle. "And we're going to take up where we left off last night!"

Laughing and straightening up, Calamity brought the team to a halt before they reached the shallow section of the stream to which she had referred. While she was applying the brake, Mark swung down from his saddle. Leaving the bloodbay "ground hitched," he bent to peer under the bed of the wagon. By the time that the red head had clambered laboriously to the ground, he had helped the lady outlaw to emerge from her place of concealment. Clad in a spoon bonnet and cheap gingham dress supplied by Calamity, who had not explained how such garments came into her possession, Belle's bruised features were grimy and streaked by perspiration. The rawhide "possum belly" was not intended to carry passengers and, despite its contents having been removed, circumstances had prevented it being cleaned adequately for occupation before she entered.

On examining Calamity and Bell after they had been bathed in the hotel's bathroom by the saloongirls, the doctor who the marshal has summoned declared that—apart from the bite on the latter's left hand—neither had suffered more than superficial injuries. In fact, such was the rugged nature of their respective constitutions, they had recovered and been coherent by the time he arrived. Each had declined the sedation she was offered to relieve the pain, claiming a good night's sleep was all she needed.

The girls had been so exhausted that, not only had the blonde slept through her removal to Mark's room, but they had both remained undisturbed by the shooting. Although he was confident that the gun play would have warned Framant against trying to reach Belle, the blond giant had decided against taking the chance of rousing her by returning her to her own bed. On being told what had happened when she

woke at five o'clock she had learned that the intruder had a
recently healed wound at the side of his head and she had
guessed his identity.

Despite being still in considerable pain, the lady outlaw
was able to think with sufficient clarity to appreciate the gravity of her situation. She knew the way in which she had
caused the fight would have aroused the suspicions of the
marshal and the bounty hunter as to her true identity, if, in-
deed, the latter was not already aware of it. Even if Framant
was deterred by the knowledge that she was under Mark's
protection, the same would not apply to Stocker. His friendship to her and the blond giant notwithstanding, he would do
his duty as a peace officer by questioning her. Having no
doubts where his intelligence and perception was concerned,
she felt sure no story she could concoct would be accepted at
face value. He might be reluctant to adopt such a course, but
he would hold her in custody while verification was sought.
Nor would telling the truth help. While it would establish she
was innocent of the bank robbery at Wichita, the disclosure
would cause her to be returned to Ellsworth to stand trial for
the successful "diamond switch" confidence trick.

Belle had been declaring her only hope of avoiding a prison
sentence was to flee, before the marshal arrived to question her
later in the morning, when a knock at the door had heralded the
arrival of Calamity. Showing admiration rather than jealousy or
annoyance over the thought that the blonde could also be contemplating love-making under the circumstances, she realized
she was in error when informed of the true state of affairs.
"Marigold Tremayne's" willingness and ability in a fight had
already earned her respect, nor was it diminished by learning she
had been up against Belle Starr. Waving aside as unimportant the
blonde's warning that aiding the escape of a person wanted by
the law was a criminal offence, she sealed what was to become a
lasting friendship by offering to help in any way she could. It
was, in fact, the red head who suggested how the departure from
Elkhorn could be achieved.[1]

After Belle had dressed and packed her portmanteau, Mark

---

1. *The new information from which we have been working in this volume suggests
the conversation took place pretty much as it was recorded in:* Part One, "The
Bounty On Belle Starr's Scalp," TROUBLED RANGE. *J.T.E.*

had taken it to Calamity's wagon and concealed it beneath the buffalo hide. Leaving the hotel when he returned to keep watch on the rooms, the red head and the blonde made the "possum belly" ready. The arrival of a hostler had prevented them from disposing of the dried buffalo chips and the logs which had been taken from it. Hearing him coming and wanting their presence to remain undiscovered, Calamity had taken shelter nearby and Belle climbed into the rawhide pouch. When it had become apparent that he intended to remain outside the livery barn, the red head had gone back to the hotel. On hearing what had happened, Mark suggested that they took their departure before the marshal could reach them. It had been their intention to clear away the discarded fuel after they had saddled and harnessed the horses, but Stocker had come upon them before this could be done. Although he had guessed what was happening, he had been willing to allow the party to leave.

"Whooee!" Calamity whooped, after having sniffed the air ostentatiously. "That's a right fetching 'par-foom' you've took to using, Belle-gal!"

"They call it '*Eau-de*-dried buffalo chips' and although I must admit it's really *you*, red top, this is the *last* time I buy any at your recommendation," the blonde replied, removing the bonnet, but her words held neither sting nor animosity and indicated a genuine liking for the person to whom they were directed. "What's more, the sooner I have a bath and get rid of it, the happier I'll be."

"Go to taking one," Mark suggested. "I'll ride circle and make sure nobody's on our trail while you do, and Calamity can take the wagon over."

"Hello the fire! Can we come ahead and make camp 'long of you?"

Having stood up on hearing the sound of a wagon approaching, Mark Counter glanced to where Calamity Jane and Belle Starr were stirring beneath their blankets.

Following the suggestions made by the blond giant, the lady outlaw had bathed in the stream and the red head attended to the needs of her wagon team while he was checking that they were not being followed. When he had rejoined them, he found Belle was wearing masculine attire produced jointly from her portmanteau and Calamity's belongings. This included a well designed gunbelt, with an unmodified Manhattan Navy revolver in its holster.

The journey had been resumed and continued uneventfully until the red head had selected the spot in which they would spend the night. As she had pointed out, she was calling the halt somewhat earlier than would have been the case if circumstances had not compelled them to leave the supply of fuel behind. Having gathered enough wood to last them until morning, Mark had left the making of the fire and cooking of a meal to the girls. With the former blazing and the latter consumed, they had bedded down—as all had done on numerous occasions—with the ground for a mattress and the sky as their ceiling. Allowing Calamity and Belle to sleep, Mark had ensured there was a good blaze maintained.

"Who-all is it?" the blond giant inquired, as Western convention permitted when such a request was made.

"Ben Lensinger and three more," the voice answered from the now stationary vehicle.

"Know him, Calam?" Mark asked.

"Sure," the red head agreed, her tone indicating a lack of cordiality. "Wouldn't say he's a friend, being choosey in my friends, but I reckon you can let him come ahead. He won't try nothing with *you* on hand."

"Come ahead," Mark authorized, advancing to toss a couple more logs in the fire so there would be added illumination with which to study the newcomers.

"That's Lensinger on the box," Calamity announced quietly and without offering to leave the blankets which were covering her, as the wagon resumed its approach to be halted on the fringe of the firelight. "Hobie Carver's driving 'n' Fred Varney's back of 'em, but I can't see the other feller."

The identity of the vehicle's fourth occupant was not long in doubt!

Although Lensinger, Carver and Varney left via the box, forming a line as soon as they reached the ground, the last member of their party made his appearance from the rear of the wagon. No sound came from Calamity, but Belle's sharp intake of breath informed Mark that—like himself—she recognized Jubal Framant. Carrying the shotgun in his right hand, grasping it by the wrist of the butt and allowing the barrels to dangle downwards, he advanced to range himself alongside Lensinger.

"Howdy, Mr. Counter," Framant greeted, standing motionless and without attempting to raise the weapon to a position of greater readiness. "We've come for Belle Starr!"

"Then you've come to the wrong place," the blond giant answered, being just as careful to avoid anything which might be construed as a hostile gesture. "There's nobody answering to her description here."

"I'm willing to *believe* she hasn't told you who she is, Mr. Counter," the bounty hunter asserted. "But we *know* that blonde gal's Belle Starr and we're making a citizen's arrest, so's we can claim that reward put out by the bank in Wichita."

"That's not why *you* want her," Mark corrected, watching Framant for the slightest warning of his intentions and relying upon the girls to keep the other men under observation. "You *know* she didn't do it."

"That's for the courts to decide, not us," the bounty hunter claimed. "We've no quarrel with *you*, just so long as you don't try to stand between us and our *legal* right to make a citizen's arrest."

"If that's what you want, come ahead," Mark replied, his voice even. "All you have to do is pass *me*!"

Which was the kind of response Framant was hoping to receive. It gave him the excuse he needed to carry out his intentions. He was confident that everything else was going as he wanted.

Neither had been aware of the other's interest, but the bounty hunter had received the information which had brought him to Elkhorn from the same person who directed Dexter Soskin there.[2] At first, so well had she changed her appearance and played her part, he was not sure whether "Marigold Tremayne" was the woman he sought. Attempting to save his own life, Wicker had claimed she was Belle Starr and this had received further verification from her behaviour in the Crystal Palace Saloon prior to the fight with Calamity Jane.

Being satisfied that he had found the woman responsible

2. *Belle Starr subsequently discovered that a clerk employed by Milton Grosvenor was augmenting his salary by selling confidential information to interested parties. However, his activities had been exposed and he had met with what appeared to be a fatal accident before she could take reprisals for the betrayal. J.T.E.*

for cheating Kramer, Framant had intended to complete his assignment while she was still in no condition to resist. However, knowing she had made the acquaintance of Mark Counter, he had considered the establishment of an alibi was essential. Fortunately for him, the means to provide one had been at hand. Having learned of the arrival in town of Jebediah Lincoln's men earlier that afternoon, he had contacted them and presented Lensinger with a letter of introduction from their employer which instructed them to supply any assistance he requested. Contacting them after the end of the fight, he had instructed them to accompany him to the room he was occupying at a small hotel. They were to stay there until the early hours of the morning and, if questioned, state he had been in their company several hours. Hearing the shooting as he was approaching the Bella Union Hotel, he had decided to call off his attempt on learning what had happened.

Guessing that the lady outlaw would leave town as soon as possible, the bounty hunter had also deduced she would be aided in her flight by the blond giant. Telling Lincoln's men that he would still require their assistance, he had silenced their protests with an assurance that he alone would go up against the Texan. He had explained that he only needed them as witnesses to support his claim of having been compelled to shoot in self defence. Such "corroboration" was essential for his future well being. As he did not know whether Dusty Fog and the Ysabel Kid were in the vicinity, he was disinclined to take the chance of killing Mark Counter and the girls, then burying their bodies and collecting the balance of his bounty from some other town. Instead, he must return to Elkhorn and establish that the Texan and the red head were gunned down while misguidedly trying to prevent the "citizen's arrest" of a wanted criminal. Even if Joel Stocker disbelieved the story, faced with the trio's "verification," his sense of duty would compel him to protect Framant against repercussions from the big blond's friends.

On deducing how his intended victim had been taken from Elkhorn, Framant had explained the advantages of following in one of Lincoln's wagons instead of being able to travel faster on horseback. His assertion that using the vehicle would enable them to approach without their true purpose being suspected had proved correct.

Now, all that remained was for the trap to be sprung!

Despite being aware that the lady outlaw and Calamity were skilled in handling revolvers, the bounty hunter did not consider they posed any undue threat. They were likely to be too stiff and sore from their recent strenuous activities to be at their best. What was more, he was confident that he would not be left to cope with them unaided. Once he had shot down the Texan, he felt sure his companions' sense of self-preservation would cause them to help deal with the girls.

Nor did Framant envisage any difficulty in playing his vitally important part in the affair. He did not doubt that the means he had employed with success in the past—including the killing of the outlaw, Wicker, two nights earlier—would prove equally effective against the blond giant. While he would have had some qualms over attempting the trick if he had been in contention against a man of Dusty Fog's proven ability as a gun fighter, he saw no reason to feel concerned in the present case.

"You mean you're defying the *law*?" the bounty hunter challenged, determined to be able to present as strong a case as possible for justifying his actions to Stocker.

"No," Mark replied. "I'm defying *you-all* and you're *not* the law!"

"So be it!" Framant declared.

Satisfied he had lulled his intended victim into a sense of false security by the way in which he was carrying his shotgun, the bounty hunter sent his left hand towards the butt of the near side revolver!

Not only did Framant believe he would take the blond giant by surprise, there was something about the weapon for which he was reaching that he considered made his success even more certain!

Because of his confidence, Framant was making a very bad error!

The bounty hunter was underestimating the man he planned to kill!

Living as he now did in the shadow of Dusty Fog's unquestioned expertise, Mark's ability as a gun fighter, and his intelligence, received little attention outside his immediate circle of acquaintances. Despite that, men in a position to *know*, considered he ran the Rio Hondo gun wizard a close second in all matters *pistolero*. Nor was he far behind his *amigo's* better publicised reputation for perception.

Immediately on seeing Framant, the blond giant had put his powers of perception into motion. Backed by his considerable experience as a gun fighter, they began to draw accurate conclusions. Remembering Belle's suppositions over the possible reason for the bounty hunter's arrival in Elkhorn, he felt sure the present visit was not merely to make a citizen's arrest and collect the reward offered by the bank at Witchita. The bounty hunter had a reputation for never taking in a living prisoner. Yet he would know the only way he could kill the lady outlaw would be after Mark was dead. Aware of who the big Texan's friends were, he would want to make it appear this was something he had been unable to avoid. Which was why he had arrived in such a fashion instead of moving in on foot and opening fire from the darkness. What was more, as he had brought along witnesses to "prove" he acted in "self defence," he could not allow Calamity to survive and give a true account of what had happened.

Realizing what was intended, Mark had wondered why Framant was carrying the shotgun in such a fashion. The moment he began to raise it into a position from which it could be fired, he would give an unmistakable warning of his intentions.

Spurred by the question, the remembrance of something which had puzzled him about the killing of Wicker struck Mark like the touch of an ice cold hand!

Why would a man armed with such a potent weapon as a shotgun endanger his life by drawing a revolver instead of using it?

Particularly as, if Framant was like the majority of men, he would have to transfer the shotgun to his left hand before he could draw the revolver!

The latter consideration provoked another!

One which might have escaped the notice of many a man!

However, not only was Mark capable of handling a Colt almost as well with either hand, he spent much of his time with Dusty Fog; who was completely ambidextrous. With such knowledge, he never discounted the possibility of an antagonist possessing an equal competence.

Furthermore, just in time, the blond giant's extensive acquaintance with firearms alerted him to another potential danger!

The butts of the bounty hunter's revolvers indicated they had not been manufactured in the factory created by Samuel Colt!

Such handles were peculiar to the arms made by Webley & Sons of Great—as it was *then*—Britain!

One of this company's best known models was the Royal Irish Constabulary, which was offered with a barrel as short as——!

Anticipating what was planned, Mark sprang to his right the instant Framant's left hand—which he had been watching instead of the one holding the shotgun—began to move. While doing so, demonstrating his unsuspected ability, he also commenced his draw.

The evasive action was only just in time!

Although carried in a holster suitable for a revolver with the dimensions of a Colt 1860 Army Model, the Webley Royal Irish Constabulary brought out by Framant had a barrel only four inches long. This allowed him to produce it with even greater ease and speed, adding to the element of surprise caused by his drawing it instead of using the shotgun.[3] However, the successes he had achieved in the past led him to be over-confident. Being so certain he had deceived his latest victim, he was caught unawares by the blond giant's action. His weapon lined and fired, sending the bullet where it was meant to go.

The trouble was, the intended target had moved!

Nor was the bounty hunter allowed to correct his error!

By the time Mark alighted from the bound which caused Framant's lead to miss and saved his life, he had both Army Colts cocked and ready in his hands. He cut loose with the

---

3. *After employing his surprise tactics, which were usually only brought into play when there were no witnesses present, Jubal Framant returned the left side Webley and, having transferred the shotgun to that hand, drew the other. This had a barrel more in keeping with the length of the holsters and, as had been the case with Marshal Joel Stocker, prevented the trick he had played from being detected. J.T.E.*

right, then the left and repeated the sequence twice more in *very* rapid succession. His bullets were directed just as accurately as the bounty hunter's had been, but with one vital difference.

When the first was fired, Framant was standing still!

Despite being jolted backwards when the first bullet tore into his body, the others followed it so quickly that all of them struck the reeling bounty hunter. Thrown from his feet, the shotgun and Webley falling from his hands, he went down. His murderous career had been brought to an end.

Nor did Lensinger fare any better. Startled by the unexpected turn of events and realizing the position in which he had been placed by allowing his support for Framant to be made obvious, he grabbed for the revolver he was wearing. Before it could clear leather, turning his way as if drawn by a magnet, the big Texan's right hand Colt sent a bullet into his head.

Sharing their companion's alarm over the way in which the situation had developed, the other two men were nevertheless slower to start taking action. What was more, as they commenced their draws, they found they were up against more than just the blond giant.

Sitting up swiftly and with a complete disregard for the pain such hurried movement created, Calamity and Belle proved to be armed and ready for action. Each held in both hands the revolver which had been beside her under the blankets, selecting and aiming at one of the remaining men from the wagon.

"Just you try it!" the red head offered grimly.

Aware of Calamity's ability and having no doubt that Belle would prove equally capable, neither Carver nor Varney was inclined to take up the challenge. Instead, they threw their hands into the air and yelled for the girls to refrain from shooting.

Hearing the drumming of rapidly approaching hooves, Mark returned the Colts to their holsters and stepped to where his Winchester lay on his blankets.

"Hello the camp!" called a familiar voice, as the blond giant was bending to pick up the rifle.

"It's Joel Stocker!" Calamity gasped.

"Why sure," the blond giant agreed. Straightening without lifting the weapon, he looked at the two men and went on grimly, "Unless you-all want to wind up in jail for attempted murder, you'd best forget who Framant told you 'Marigold' there is. If you so much as *hint* at it, I'll swear it was you pair who threatened to kill us all and, by god, I'll make it stick!"

"Looks like I got here a mite too late," the peace officer remarked on his arrival, having dismounted by the wagon and looked around. "When I heard Framant'd left town in a wagon with these three, I reckoned he could've been lying about not being after 'Miss Marigold' and came along to find out why. Do *you* know?"

"N—No!" replied Varney, to whom the question had been directed. Thinking fast, he came up with what he hoped would be an acceptable explanation for his presence, one which could not be disputed provided his companion gave him backing. "Ben there said's he'd hired us, but didn't tell us why. Did he, Hobie?"

"He just said we was to come along and lend a hand should it be needed," Carver confirmed, although his tone lacked conviction. "We didn't know what they was up to."

"Perhaps he mistook one of us for somebody he'd seen on a wanted poster, marshal?" Belle offered.

"I'll be danged if I can figure out which of you that'd be, 'Miss Marigold,'" Stocker asserted blandly. "*None* of you matches a description I've seen on *any* wanted dodger that's passed through my hands. Anyways, even if you did, this's out of my bailiwick. I just come out to try to stop Framant having to shoot somebody else in 'self defence' and, seeing's how he won't be doing it again, I'm satisfied. You jaspers load them two on the wagon and take them back to Elkhorn. Happen you folks don't mind, I'll bed down here with you and head back comes morning."

"We don't mind," Mark affirmed and the girls nodded concurrence. "It'll let me get a good night's sleep for a change."

"I know you missed one *last* night, Mark," Belle commented in her innocent fashion. "But I can't imagine how you did the night before."

"Or the night afore that, either," Calamity Jane declared.

"Don't ask me *how*," Mark grinned. "I only know I *did* and I didn't mind at all."[4]

---

4. *As a result of the information Belle Starr supplied to Milton Grosvenor, newly appointed United States' Marshal Solomon Wisdom "Solly" Cole was sent as his first assignment to investigate the robbery of the bank at Wichita. He ascertained that it was planned by a dishonest bank teller and a saloongirl. Having tricked four young men into helping, they had left the money with her before fleeing and the teller accompanied the posse to ensure none of them survived. It was the girl who was seen, wearing a disguise, then started the rumor that the "gang's" accomplice was Belle Starr. U.S. Marshal Cole makes "guest" appearances in the* Calamity Jane *sections of* J.T.'S HUNDREDTH *and* J.T.'S LADIES, *also in* CALAMITY SPELLS TROUBLE. *J.T.E.*

Deserted by her husband, Charlotte Canary decided the best way she could ensure a safe future for her children was to leave them in a St. Louis' convent and head west to seek her fortune. However, there had been too much of her lively and reckless spirit in her eldest daughter, Martha Jane, for the scheme to be entirely successful. Rebelling against the strict life imposed by the nuns, the girl celebrated her birthday by running away. Hiding in one of Cecil "Dobe" Killem's freight wagons, she had traveled some twelve miles from the city before being discovered. She might have been sent back to the convent, but the cook was found to be too drunk to work. One of the things which the girl had learned from the nuns was good, plain cooking. The meal she had prepared was so satisfactory Killem yielded to her request to be taken to Wichita, Kansas, where she claimed she had an aunt who would give her a home.

Before the outfit had reached its destination, raiding Sioux warriors who wiped out two other freight outfits failed to locate them. What was more, the goods they were carrying had been sold so advantageously that the whole crew received a bonus and their employer was offered a lucrative contract to deliver supplies further west. Learning that the aunt was a figment of the girl's imagination and having come to regard her as a good luck charm, the drivers had prevailed upon Killem to let her stay with them. Not that he, having taken a liking to her for her spunk and cheerful nature, had taken much persuading.

At first, Martha had helped the cook and, wearing male clothing for convenience, carried out other menial duties. She soon graduated to driving and, learning fast, in a short while there was little she could not do in that line of work. Not only could she harness and drive a Conestoga wagon's six horse team, she carried out the vehicle's maintenance to Killem's exacting requirements. She was taught to use a long lashed bull whip as an inducement to equestrian activity, or as an effective weapon, to handle firearms and generally take care of herself upon the open ranges of the West. Nor did her self reliance end there. Visiting saloons along with the rest of the outfit, she had frequently been called upon to defend herself against the objections of the female denizens who resented her trespassing on their domain. Although the lady outlaw, Belle Starr, *q.v.*, held her to a hard fought draw when they first met, leading a much more active and healthy life than the saloon-girls, she was only beaten once.[1]

Courageous, loyal to her friends, happy go lucky and generous to such an extent she deliberately lost a saloon she had inherited jointly with a professional gambler, Frank Derringer,[2] the girl had a penchant for becoming involved in dangerous and precarious situations. Visiting New Orleans, she had acted as a decoy to lure the Strangler—a notorious mass murderer of young women—to his doom.[3] While delivering supplies to an Army post, she fought with a female professional pugilist and helped to rescue a cavalry officer captured by Indians.[4] In Texas, she had helped wipe out a wave of cattle stealing which was threatening to cause a range war.[5] What started out as a peaceful journey as a passenger on a stagecoach ended with her being compelled to take over as driver and take part in the capture of outlaws who robbed it.[6] Going to visit a ranch which had been left to her by her father, accompanied by the Ysabel Kid, *q.v.*, she was nearly killed when a rival claimant had her fastened to a log which was being sent through a circular saw.[7] She had also played a major part in averting an Indian uprising in Canada in the company of Belle "the Rebel Spy" Boyd[8] and a British Secret Service agent, Captain Patrick "the Remittance Kid" Reeder.[9] During a big game hunt with a visiting British sportsman and his sister, she was kidnapped.[10]

Among her friends, she counted the members of the OD Connected's floating outfit, *q.v.*, being on particularly intimate terms with Mark Counter.[11] She also, on one memorable occasion, posed as the wife of its leader, Captain Dustine Edward Marsden "Dusty" Fog, *q.v.*, assisting to deal with a band of land grabbers.[12] Other close acquaintances were James Butler "Wild Bill" Hickok and his wife, Agnes,[13] and she captured his murderer on the day he was killed.[14]

Because of her penchant for finding trouble and becoming involved in brawls, the girl soon acquired the sobriquet by which she became famous throughout the West and beyond.

People called her "Calamity Jane."

FOOTNOTES

1. The story of how the defeat came about is told in, Part One, "Better Than Calamity," THE WILDCATS.

2. Told in: COLD DECK, HOT LEAD. *Further Details of Frank Derringer's career are given in:* QUIET TOWN, THE MAKING OF A LAWMAN, THE TROUBLE BUSTERS *and* THE GENTLE GIANT.

3. Told in: THE BULL WHIP BREED.

4. Told in: TROUBLE TRAIL.

5. Told in: THE COW THIEVES.

6. Told in: CALAMITY SPELLS TROUBLE.

7. Told in: WHITE STALLION, RED MARE.

8. Told in: THE WHIP AND THE WAR LANCE. *Further details of Belle "the Rebel Spy's" career are given in:* THE COLT AND THE SABRE; THE REBEL SPY; THE BAD BUNCH; THE HOODED RIDERS; Part Eight, "Affair of Honour," J.T.'S HUNDREDTH; TO ARMS! TO ARMS! IN DIXIE!; THE SOUTH WILL RISE AGAIN; SET A-FOOT; THE QUEST FOR BOWIE'S BLADE; THE REMITTANCE KID *and* Part Five, "The Butcher's Fiery End," J.T.'S LADIES.

9. The researches of fictionist genealogist Philip Jose Farmer, q.v., have established that Captain (later Major General Sir) Patrick "the Remittance Kid" Reeder (K.C.B., V.C., D.S.O., M.C. and Bar) was the uncle of the celebrated British detective, Mr. J.G. Reeder, whose biography is recorded in: ROOM 13, THE MIND OF MR. J.G. REEDER, RED ACES, MR. J.G. REEDER RETURNS *and* TERROR KEEP, *by Edgar Wallace, and whose organization played a prominent part in the events described in our* "CAP" FOG, TEXAS RANGER, MEET MR. J. G. REEDER.

10. Told in: THE BIG HUNT.

11. See Footnote 14, APPENDIX TWO for details of other meetings between Miss Canary and Mark Counter.

12. Told in: Part Two, "A Wife For Dusty Fog," THE SMALL TEXAN.

13. One meeting between Miss Canary and Mrs. Agnes Hickok is described in, Part Six, "Mrs. Wild Bill," J.T.'S LADIES.

14. Told in: Part Seven, "Deadwood, August 2nd, 1876," J.T.'S HUNDREDTH.

APPENDIX TWO

With his exceptional good looks and magnificent physical development,[1] Mark Counter presented the kind of physical appearance many people expected of his *amigo*, Captain Dustine Edward Marsden "Dusty" Fog.[2] It was a fact of which they took advantage when the need arose.[3] On one occasion, it was the cause of the blond giant being subjected to a murder attempt although the Rio Hondo gun wizard was intended as the victim.[4]

While serving as a lieutenant under General Bushrod Sheldon's command during the War Between The States, Mark's merits as an efficient and courageous officer had been overshadowed by his unconventional taste in uniforms. Always something of a dandy, coming from a wealthy family had allowed him to indulge his whims. Despite considerable opposition and disapproval on the part of hide-bound senior officers, his selection of a "skirtless" tunic in particular had come to be much copied by the other young bloods of the Confederate States' Army.[5] Similarly in later years, having been given independent means via the will of a maiden aunt,[6] his taste in attire had dictated what the well dressed Texas' cowhand would wear to be in fashion.

When peace had come, Mark accompanied Sheldon to Mexico to fight Emperor Maximilian. There he met Dusty Fog and the Ysabel Kid, helping the small Texan to accomplish a mission upon which the future relations between the United States of America and Mexico hung in the balance.[7] On returning to Texas, he had been invited to work for Dusty's uncle—General Jackson Baines "Ole Devil" Hardin, C.S.A., Rtd.[8]—as a member of the OD Connected ranch's floating outfit.[9] Knowing his two elder brothers could help his father, Big Rance, to run the family's R Over C ranch in the Big Bend country—and suspecting life would be more exciting in the company of his two *amigos*—he had accepted.

An expert cowhand, Mark had become known a Dusty's right bower.[10] He had also gained acclaim by virtue of his enormous strength and ability in a bare handed roughhouse brawl. However, due to being so much in the company of the Rio Hondo gun wizard, his full potential as a gun fighter received little attention. Men who were competent to judge such matters stated that, whether with a brace of Colt 1860 Army Model revolvers[11] or their successors, the Cavalry Model Peacemaker,[12] he was second only to the small Texan in speed and accuracy.[13]

Many women found Mark irresistible, including Miss Martha "Calamity Jane" Canary.[14] However, in his younger days, only one—the lady outlaw, Belle Starr[15]—held his heart.[16] It was not until several years after Belle's death that he courted and married Dawn Sutherland, who he had first met on the trail drive taken by Colonel Charles Goodnight to Fort Sumner, New Mexico.[17] The discovery of oil on their ranch brought an added wealth to them and this commodity now forms the major part of the present day members of the family's income.[18]

FOOTNOTES

1. *Two of Mark Counter's great grandsons, Deputy Sheriff Bradford "Brad" Counter and James Allenvale "Bunduki" Gunn inherited his looks and physique. They also have achieved considerable fame on their respective behalf. Details of the former's career as a peace officer are given in the* Rockabye County *series, covering various aspects of law enforcement in present day Texas. Much of the latter's life is recorded in,* Part Twelve, "The Mchawi's Powers," J.T.'S HUNDREDTH *and the volumes of the* Bunduki *series.*

2. *Although our earlier source suggested Captain Dustine Edward Marsden "Dusty" Fog and the Ysabel Kid arrived shortly after the gun fight and a different principal contender was involved, the actual meeting occurred later in Belle Starr's journey to safety. Details of Dusty's and the Kid's special qualifications and backgrounds are given in various volumes of the* Civil War *and* Floating Outfit *series. J.T.E.*

   3. *One occasion is recorded in:* THE SOUTH WILL RISE AGAIN.

   4. The incident is recorded in: BEGUINAGE.

   5. The Manual of Dress Regulations *for the Army of the Confederate States*

stipulated that the tunic should have a *"skirt extending to half way between hip and knee."*

6. One result of the bequest is described in: Part Two, The Floating Outfit series (Mark Counter) in "We Hang Horse Thieves High," J.T.'S HUNDREDTH.

7. Told in: THE YSABEL KID.

8. Details of General Jackson Baines "Ole Devil" Hardin's career are given in the Ole Devil Hardin and Civil War series. How he was crippled and left confined to a wheelchair shortly after his retirement from the Army of the Confederate States is told in: Part Three, "The Paint," THE FASTEST GUN IN TEXAS and his death is reported in: DOC LEROY, M.D.

9. "Floating outfit": a group of from four to six cowhands employed by a large ranch to work the more distant sections of its range. Taking food in a chuck wagon, or "greasy sack" on the back of a mule, they would be away from the ranch house for several days at a time. For that reason, they were selected from the best and most trustworthy members of the crew. Because of General Hardin's prominence in the affairs of Texas, the OD Connected's floating outfit were frequently sent to assist such of his friends who found themselves in difficulty or endangered.

10. "Right bower": second in command, derived from the title of the second highest trump card in the game of euchre.

11. Although the military sometimes claimed derisively it was easier to kill a sailor than a soldier, the weight factor of the respective weapons caused the United States' Navy to adopt a revolver of .36 caliber while the Army employed the heavier .44. The weapon would be carried on a seaman's belt and not—handguns having originally and primarily been developed for use by cavalry—on the person or the saddle of a man who did all his traveling and fighting from the back of a horse. Therefore, .44 became known as the "Army" calibre and .36 as the "Navy." Although the Colt 1860 Army Model revolvers intended primarily for sale to the military had barrels of eight inches in length, those manufactured for the civilian market were half an inch shorter.

12. Introduced in 1873, as the Colt Model P "Single Action Army" revolver, originally with a caliber of .45, it was more popularly known as the "Peacemaker." Production continued until 1941, when it was taken out of the line to make way for the more modern weapons required in World War II. Over three hundred and fifty thousand were manufactured in practically every handgun caliber—with the exception of the .41 and .44 Magnums which were not developed during the period of manufacture—from .22 Short Rimfire to .476 Eley. Those chambered .44.40 were given the name, "Frontier Model" and handled the same cartridge as the Winchester Model of 1873 rifle and carbine. Popular demand, said to have been caused by the upsurge of action-escapism-adventure Western series on television brought the Peacemaker back into production in 1955 and it is still in the line.

12a. The barrel lengths of the Model P could be from three inches in the "Storekeeper" Model, which did not have an extractor rod, to the sixteen inches of the so-called "Buntline Special." The latter was also offered with an attachable metal "skeleton" butt stock so it could be used as an extemporized carbine. However, the main barrel lengths were: Cavalry Model, seven and a half inches; Artillery Model, five and a half; Civilian Model, four and three quarters.

13. Evidence of Mark Counter's competence as a gun fighter and his standing in comparison with Dusty Fog is given in: TRIGGER FAST.

14. Miss Martha "Calamity Jane" Canary's other meetings with Mark Counter are described in: Part One, "The Bounty On Belle Starr's Scalp," TROUBLED RANGE—upon which this work is an expansion—Part One, "Better Than Calam-

ity," THE WILDCATS, CUT ONE, THEY ALL BLEED, THE BAD BUNCH, THE FORTUNE HUNTERS, THE BIG HUNT, GUNS IN THE NIGHT.

15. *We are frequently asked why it is the Belle Starr we describe is so different from photographs which appear in various books. The researches of fictionist-genealogist Philip José Farmer—author of, among numerous other works, the incomparable* TARZAN ALIVE, A Definitive Biography of Lord Greystoke *and* DOC SAVAGE, His Apocalyptic *Life—with whom we consulted have established that the "Belle Starr" we describe is not the same person as another equally famous bearer of the name. However, the Counter family have asked that we and Mr. Farmer keep her true identity a secret and we intend to do so.*

16. *How Mark Counter's romance with Belle Starr progressed after the events recorded in this volume is given in* RANGELAND HERCULES, THE BAD BUNCH, *Mark's section of* J.T.'S HUNDREDTH, *q.v.,* THE GENTLE GIANT, Part Four, Mark Counter in "A Lady Known as Belle," THE HARD RIDERS *and how it ended is described in:* GUNS IN THE NIGHT. *Belle also makes "guest" appearances in:* HELL IN THE PALO DURO, GO BACK TO HELL *and* THE QUEST FOR BOWIE'S BLADE.

17. *Told in:* GOODNIGHT'S DREAM (*U.S.A. Bantam Books 1974 Edition re-titled* THE FLOATING OUTFIT) *and* FROM HIDE AND HORN.

18. *This is established by inference in:* Case Three, "The Deadly Ghost," YOU'RE A TEXAS RANGER, ALVIN FOG.

THE END

203